WEST END GIRL

It's 1901 and Lizzie and her family are working at Glasgow's International Exhibition. While selling tickets, Lizzie rescues Alice from attack by her moody, dangerous fiancé, Charles. As Lizzie and Alice's friendship deepens so does the danger posed by Charles, especially as Alice has fallen in love with William, one of his employees. Lizzie meets gondolier, Jamie, and falls in love. It will take all four of them to survive the terrible events which unfold when the Exhibition finally shuts its gates.

CAROL MacLEAN

◆

WEST END GIRL

Complete and Unabridged

LINFORD
ROMANCE

LINFORD
Leicester

First published in Great Britain in 2020

First Linford Edition
published 2021

A catalogue record for this book is available
from the British Library.

ISBN 978–1–4448–4730–7

Published by
Ulverscroft Limited
Anstey, Leicestershire

Printed and bound in Great Britain by
T J Books Ltd., Padstow, Cornwall

This book is printed on acid-free paper

1

Glasgow 1901

Lizzie noticed the girl's hat first. It was a rather beautiful confection with sea-blue gauze ribbons and pretty posies of pale blue flowers. It matched her neat jacket and long navy skirt. Her hair and face by contrast were quite ordinary. For a brief moment, Lizzie felt disappointed. Surely, such a wonderful hat deserved a beautiful owner. As she glanced a second time, she was struck by how still the girl was, in amongst the bustling crowd and the noise of excited visitors. She was sitting painting, an easel in front of her and a large leather bag at her side. People swarmed on either side of her, parting around the small figure like a large, colourful river.

'Look where you're going!'

A large woman with two small boys barged past her, glaring and muttering.

'Sorry,' Lizzie said. When she looked back the girl was no longer visible. A marching band was going past slowly, brass instruments gleaming in the sunlight. A few minutes more and she'd forgotten all about the hat and its owner. Caught up in the crowd she was being moved in the direction of the Palace of Industry with its glittering golden dome and snowy white walls.

It was July, and Glasgow was two months into holding the Great International Exhibition of 1901 at Kelvingrove Park. The centrepiece of the exhibition was the impressive Palace of Industry, which was constructed of plaster and wood and would be taken down at the end of the exhibition, leaving nothing but memories. However, at this moment, no-one was thinking ahead to November and instead, everyone's minds were focused entirely on the fun and amazing spectacles to be seen daily at such a wonderful place.

Lizzie loved it all. To the people working there and those living locally, the

Exhibition was known fondly as the Groveries due perhaps to the secret groves of plants and ferneries scattered around the area or some said it was taken from the name of the grand park itself.

Just inside the entrance hall on the left was a café.

Mrs Morgan's Meeting Room was cheerfully painted in buttercup yellow and held a scattering of circular tables at which groups and pairs of ladies were taking tea and nibbling on tiny cakes. Two waitresses in white blouses and grey skirts were taking orders.

Mrs Morgan waved to Lizzie from her position behind the counter.

'Hello dear. Cup of tea or do you want to go on through?'

'I'm here to see Ma, if you don't mind. I won't keep her long,' Lizzie said politely. She slid in behind the counter and through a door into the back of the café.

A tired looking woman was washing dishes at a sink. The child, standing beside her, squealed when she glimpsed

Lizzie, threw down her tea towel and hugged her fiercely around the waist.

Lizzie dropped a kiss on her sister's head.

'Are you taking me to see the Russians?' Iona asked, excitedly.

'Not today, darling. Maybe tomorrow.'

Iona's face fell. She pouted. 'You always say that and you never do. I hate you Lizzie MacDonald.' She stamped a foot and turned her back.

'Now, Iona, there's no call for that kind of behaviour,' her mother said gently.

Lizzie saw that her hands were raw red and chapped. It hurt her to look at them. If only she had a better job, then Ma wouldn't have to work so hard. She watched as Ma winced and rubbed her painful hip. An accident at the farm where she'd grown up had left her with a lifelong limp. Standing for hours washing plates and cups and cutlery was doing her no good.

'We're lucky we've got work,' Mary said, seeing Lizzie's expression. 'Just remember that. It's all very well dreaming but we have to eat.'

'I wish … ' Lizzie sighed.

'That's what I mean, my love. Your head's in the clouds. Come down to reality. Why are you here? Shouldn't you be giving out the leaflets?'

'I've given them all out. I'm on my way to find Mr Barrow to get some more.'

'And the café is on the way?' Mary asked, knowing fine well that it wasn't.

Lizzie flushed. It was as close to a reprove as Ma would make.

'I found a little bird with a broken wing. I need a box and a towel to make a nest for it.'

Mary gave a sweet smile. 'My Lizzie with the big heart. It'll bring you trouble some day, you know. You can't care for the world.'

'It's one wee bird, Ma. That's all.'

'And before that, the lambs that wouldn't suckle, the blackbird with the crooked bill and a dozen other creatures that nature would've taken care of itself.' But Mary's tone was warm with humour. Then she sighed.

Lizzie knew what she was thinking of. Their home in the Scottish Highlands. A tiny blackhouse in the wild countryside of the estate. There was a hunting lodge for the laird and his lady, a home farm and shepherds' cottages. It was a good place to grow up, with the fresh air and plentiful food for the estate workers.

Mrs Morgan's head appeared around the door.

'We need clean cups and saucers, Mary.'

'Of course, just coming. Iona, take these cups out to the counter,' Mary said hurriedly, pushing her younger daughter to the sink.

Mrs Morgan disappeared in a rustle of lilac bombazine.

'Here, take this wooden crate, she won't miss it. And this towel, it's threadbare any way. Hurry away, I can't afford to lose this job, as you well know. Mrs Morgan is a kind lady but she won't tolerate slackness.'

Their gazes met in mutual understanding. Lizzie nodded and grabbed the box and towel. But by the time she'd made her way back to the street where she had seen the sparrow it was all over. She stroked its soft feathers sadly. Its body was stiff and its eyes dulled.

'What you got there?' Two scruffy boys stared at her and one of them poked the bird with a stick. She shooed them away. She put the little body into the box and hid it under the towel. She'd give it a Christian burial. It was the least she could do. Her eyes welled up and she squeezed them shut to stop the easy tears.

The box under her arm, she walked swiftly to Mr Barrow's stall which was almost at the entrance to Kelvingrove Park and the International Exhibition. She heard his bellowing roar before she got there.

'Roll up, roll up! Get your tickets here. Find out what pleasures await you tomorrow at the biggest and the best Exhibition in this new century and at His Majesty's command.'

Lizzie hid a smile. Mr Barrow, bright

and unmissable in his candy-striped waistcoat and with his bowler hat tipped back from a shiny bald head, saw her and frowned. He continued to bellow encouragement to the crowds of sight-seers as she tucked the box under the stall table and grabbed a large handful of leaflets. Before he could complain about where she had been, she was off again.

It wasn't a well paid job but giving out leaflets and selling tickets meant that she had the freedom to roam the entire Exhibition, or the Groveries as it was known by the locals and the large number of people who worked there. Covering seventy-three hectares of ground, there was a lot to see. The main attraction was the Palace of Industry, specially built for the Exhibition and rumour had it that it would be dismantled at the end of it. Lizzie didn't believe that. It looked built to last. Of course there was also the splendid new red sandstone Art Gallery and Museum, filled, it was said, with priceless paintings. Lizzie didn't know because she hadn't been inside, despite it being free entry every day. It said so on Mr Barrow's extravagant leaflets.

Beyond the white palace was an entire Russian village with seven halls full of mysterious displays and a stage at which exotic dancers and acrobats performed. There was a full working dairy farm and a great Hall of Machinery on the other side of the road. A covered walkway joined the machinery hall to the rest of the Exhibition. There was a miniature railway and a great water shute into the River Kelvin. But Lizzie's favourites were the gondolas, punted by Italian gondoliers. They were so romantic, she thought with a deep sigh of delight. She liked to go and wander along the river's edge just to hear the strange, melodic voices with their foreign words. It didn't matter that she couldn't understand them. Working at the Exhibition was like travelling abroad. Except that the world had come to Glasgow. As she wandered through the site, she heard many different accents and languages and saw people wearing strange costumes.

'I hear that the King of Siam is coming to visit,' she heard a man telling his wife.

Lizzie's hand flew to her chest. How wonderful that would be. Imagine if she saw him. It would be a memory to last a lifetime. She was humming a tune under her breath when a flash of blue caught the corner of her eye.

She had reached a quiet area, far from the busy palace. It was a park with a stone fountain and groves of trees. Families strolled and a nanny pushed a baby's perambulator along a path. It was Lizzie's familiar route to the River Kelvin and the gondolas.

Behind a thicket of bushes, two figures were struggling. A tall man, dressed in black towered over a smaller figure. Strangely, they made no sound. Lizzie gasped as she recognised the girl with the blue hat. The hat had been knocked awry and pale brown hair was visible along with a shocked white face. For a moment Lizzie was rooted to the ground. Then she dropped her leaflets and ran towards them.

'What are you doing?' she cried. She stumbled, her legs tangled in her long skirt and took a moment to right herself.

The man looked up, his hand gripping his victim's upper arm. Lizzie almost froze at his expression. It was dark and cruel and his stare seemed to take everything about her in, as if he had marked her physically. She shivered but forced herself forward. He let go of the girl and Lizzie heard a faint moan as she fainted. The man brushed past her as she ran the last few feet to where the girl lay. She smelt a whiff of fine cologne and cigar smoke and then he was gone.

'Are you hurt? Can you hear me?' she said, kneeling beside the girl.

Giving another low moan, the girl's eyes flickered open.

'Is he gone?' she whispered.

'Yes, you have nothing to fear,' Lizzie said, more confidently than she felt. She glanced over her shoulder, half expecting to see him return to assault them both. But there was no-one there.

'Can you sit up?' She supported the girl's shoulders as she tried to raise her head.

Soon, she was sitting up. Lizzie kept her arm around her.

'We should call for the police.'

'No, no, we mustn't. Promise me you will not?'

She had an educated accent and Lizzie had been right about the quality of her clothes. What was a wealthy young lady doing alone at the Exhibition? Lizzie knew enough about the moneyed classes to know that young ladies had chaperones.

'Are you certain? Do you know that man?' Lizzie asked doubtfully.

'He is my fiancé.'

Her lips trembled and she began to sob quietly. Lizzie felt her thin shoulders shudder with the crying. The beautiful blue hat was soiled from the struggle and one of the gauzy ribbons was torn. A button was missing from the top of her jacket.

Her face was chalky and her lips almost

bloodless. There were dark shadows under her eyes. Beside her, with her pink cheeks and thick red hair, Lizzie seemed obscenely full of life. Even their hands showed the contrast. The girl's were pale with prominent blue veins while Lizzie's were brown from the sun.

'My name is Alice Whittaker. And you are?' the girl whispered, as if they had met in a parlour somewhere.

'Lizzie MacDonald. Would you like a drink? Shall we sit at the café across the park?'

'Yes, please. Where … where's my bag? My easel?'

Lizzie stood up and searched. Beyond the shrubbery, she found them. Thrown carelessly aside. She imagined the man throwing them away contemptuously. She picked them up and took them back to Alice.

They walked slowly over to a café on the other side of the park land. Although it was now late afternoon, the sun was still warm and high in the sky. A family with four young children sat at one

13

table, laughing and chatting. At another, a group of young gentlemen sat, arguing about something in a well mannered fashion. Alice sat down stiffly, leaving Lizzie to order two coffees. They didn't speak until the drinks had arrived and they had sipped them eagerly.

'Do you want to tell me what happened?' Lizzie said finally.

Alice sipped her drink a little longer before putting the cup gently back into its saucer. There was a slight clink of china as her hand wobbled.

'I am engaged to Mr Charles Tunbridge. I have been engaged for two years and he is losing patience. He is a widower and he wants an heir.' Alice broke off with a shuddering sigh.

Lizzie pressed her hand in sympathy. It was unbelievable that her fiancé had attacked her! What kind of man could he be?

'I have been ill for the past two years and I'm recuperating. My Mama doesn't want me to marry until I am quite well. While Father ... Well, in any case, I don't wish to marry Mr Tunbridge at all.'

Alice sat back, her lips pressed firmly together. Lizzie was surprised. For such a frail creature, it looked as if Alice had some backbone after all. She felt the beginnings of admiration for her. She also wondered what it was that the awful Mr Tunbridge saw in her. For Alice was quite plain. Her hair was a soft, mousey brown and her eyes a dull grey. Her features were even and pleasant but by no means pretty. She was too thin to be fashionable. She looked sickly.

'Where is your Mama?' Lizzie asked, finishing the dregs of her coffee and finding them still tasty.

'Oh, Mama is not in Glasgow. She is visiting with relatives in London. No, I am in the care of my Aunt Hilda for the duration. She is, unfortunately, given to gossiping with her acquaintances and so I am left to my own devices every day.'

'Do you come to the Exhibition every day?' Lizzie said, her eyebrows rising.

'I have a season ticket so that I can come every day. I live near the Kelvingrove and I can look at the Exhibition from my bedroom window. It is so fascinating. Father says I may come here with Aunt Hilda and spend my time sketching and painting.'

Lizzie stared at her the way she might an interesting insect or bird. What would it be like to have so much free time every day that one might spend it all painting or simply watching the shows? Not to have to work every day and worry about whether there was enough to eat and what the next day or week or month might bring. It was a different life for the gentry, that was for sure.

There was a pause in the conversation while Alice drank her coffee. She was no longer shaking and now she attempted to tidy her hair, stroking its strands back behind her ears and retying her ribbon as best she could.

'What do you think Mr Tunbridge was trying to do back there?' Lizzie said, carefully.

'To compromise me, so that we should have to marry in haste.'

'Can he not wait for marriage until you are quite well again?'

'Mr Tunbridge is not a patient man. He is used to getting his own way. To be thwarted by a young woman is galling to him.'

'Are you thwarting him?'

'Those are his words, not mine,' Alice said wearily.

She looked tired and Lizzie worried that she might faint once more. Alice's bag was beside her, its clasp undone. She went to close it but a corner of one of the paintings was visible. She took it out. It was a sketch of Indian dancers, delicately painted with watercolours.

'This is very good,' she said. 'You are very talented.'

'It whiles away the hours,' Alice said with a faint smile. 'Whether it is good or not, I have no idea. There is no-one to discuss such matters with.'

'Your mother and father?' Lizzie thought about her own family. They talked and argued about everything. It was impossible to keep anything to herself. She had often wished for peace to think. But loneliness such as Alice's she did not envy.

'Do you paint?' Alice asked.

Lizzie laughed. 'There's not much chance of that. I'm too busy to be able to sit and paint. Besides, I couldn't afford the brushes and colours. I can draw a little, if I can get the paper.'

Alice stared at her as if seeing her properly for the first time. Lizzie knew she couldn't match Alice's elegance. She was wearing her only skirt, faded green cotton, with a blouse that was threadbare with too many scrubbings. She had no hat or gloves and her hobnail boots were hand-me-downs from her brother Donald.

'Pass me my bag,' Alice said suddenly.

From its depths, she produced a black stick and a fresh sheet of creamy paper.

'Here.' She thrust them at Lizzie. 'Draw for me.'

The black stick made soft, easy marks on the paper. It smeared easily too. But what to draw? She took a few minutes to sketch and then passed the paper back to Alice, who clapped her hands.

'Wonderful.' She smiled. 'It's me and you've caught the shape of my hat so well. I can almost visualise the blue colours.'

In the distance a band began to play. People were leaving the café and heading for the central palace. Lizzie jumped up, suddenly conscious that she was meant to be working. Mr Barrow would be after her if he found her sitting drinking coffee when she should be handing out his special leaflets. There were tickets for tonight's shows to be sold too.

'I've got to go.'

'Oh, please don't!' Alice exclaimed. 'Stay and talk. There's so much to discuss.'

'I'm sorry, I can't. I'm working.'

'At least say we can meet again? We can sit and paint together. I'll lend you paper and watercolours.'

'I'll find you,' Lizzie said. 'If you're here every day, I'll see you somewhere. I'm all over the Exhibition. Now, will you be alright? Do you want me to walk you anywhere?' She was impatient to be gone. No doubt Mr Barrow had a queue of others desperate to take her job.

'I can find my own way. Thank you, Lizzie.'

Lizzie tried to ignore the disappointment in Alice's voice.

'Goodbye, then.'

She didn't look back but felt Alice's sad gaze between her shoulder blades every step of the way until she was out of sight and running downhill to Mr Barrow's stall.

'Where the heck have you been?' he bellowed, his face ruddy with displeasure. 'There's tickets waiting. If you haven't sold them all by dinner, you needn't show up tomorrow. You hear me?'

'Sorry, Mr Barrow. There was an accident. I had to help.'

He wasn't listening. He had turned with an oily grin to a well dressed dowager and was pressing complimentary tickets into her gloved hand with a low bow. Lizzie made a face as she hunkered down to pick up the box with the dead bird. She could sell tickets on her way to the river and then bury the poor little thing.

Box tucked under her arm and a tray of tickets slung around her neck, she set off in the direction of the river. She shouted out as she went, enticing people to buy tickets for the various shows that night. Her strong, piercing voice was the main reason Mr Barrow had hired her over two young men also desperate for the job. That, and the fact that she wasn't Irish like them.

'I don't usually take on your lot either,' he told her. 'Taking the food out of Glasgow mouths, and there's more and more of you infesting our fine city, but you've got a pair of good lungs and I won't employ the Irish. Worse than dogs and fleas they are.'

Lizzie had to bite her tongue and lower her eyes modestly. Inside, she was raging. Who did Mr Bellow think made the railway that he proudly travelled on each day to the Exhibition? Who had built the

21

palace of arts? Or the covered walkway or the working dairy farm? Without the immigrants, Glasgow would be a poorer city by far. All this, Lizzie thought but didn't say. She needed the work so she had to swallow her pride, as Mary said when she told her later what Mr Barrow had said.

The River Kelvin was dark and smelly but somehow, with the coming of the Exhibition, it had gained a romantic aura. She heard the screams of delight as a boat full of people went down the giant water shute and the splashes as they shot through the river water.

She had sold but half her tickets. Lizzie shrugged. She could sell the rest on her way back. She walked along to the river side, gazing at the gondolas. The gondoliers stood at the back of the long boats, punting them along with a pole and singing in Italian. There was a wooden landing stage and a couple of the gondoliers stood there, waiting for customers.

It was busy on the path alongside the river. The smell of oil and weed and waste rose to her nostrils as people brushed past her, intent on pleasure and getting the most from the sunny day. She was thinking about where to bury the bird and enjoying the feel of the sun on her hair when she felt a blow to her back. Suddenly she was falling towards the water, the box spinning away and the tickets spraying every which way across the grassy slope.

She came up choking. Her hair was plastered to her face and for a moment she couldn't see. Then her arms spun wildly as she tried to get a grip of the earth. She was in the river and the water was cold and her clothes were dragging her down into the black depths. She opened her mouth to take another breath and tasted water. She was sinking.

Just as panic set in and she was sure she was drowning, she felt strong hands under her armpits. The water was drawn away from her. Then she was on the river bank, on hands and knees, retching up the dirty water. A ring of feet surrounded her. She saw good leather, soft kid slippers and bare toes as her head spun. She squeezed her eyes shut.

When she opened them again, the feet had gone except for one pair. The same strong hands pulled her up, not unkindly. She was horribly aware of her soaked blouse and the curve of her breasts on show. Her skirt clung to her legs too. Her legs gave way and she sat heavily onto the river bank. A moment later, a jacket was slung around her shoulders. She hugged it gratefully.

'Better?' a deep voice asked her.

She looked up. A gondolier stood over her. It was his jacket she was wearing.

'Now, will you tell me, why anyone would want to push you into the river?' he said.

2

Lizzie coughed and tasted river water at the back of her throat.

'Are you going to spew again?'

She shook her head.

'Good.'

She shivered despite the sunshine and pulled the jacket to her. Her hair hung in fat, wet tails, dripping down her back. It didn't matter because her clothes were sodden.

'Can I take you anywhere?' the gondolier said. 'You need to get dry before you catch a chill. Drinking the river isn't a good idea.'

'Thank you,' she said, looking up at him, 'For saving me. I can't swim.' For a moment she relived the moment when she began to sink and shivered even more as she realised she could have drowned.

'Best keep my jacket to get you home. You can bring it back tomorrow,' he said.

'You're not Italian,' Lizzie said, looking at him properly.

He had thick, brown hair and dark brown eyes. His face and bare arms were as tanned as any Italian but his strong local accent gave him away. He gave her a cheeky grin.

'You've found me out.'

'I thought all the gondoliers were,' she said, feeling cheated in a odd way as her romantic vision of the gondolas on the river evaporated.

'Most of them are. If you had taken a punt down the river on my gondola, you'd never have known the difference. I can sing in Italian and I get by talking on a few phrases my friend Frederico has taught me. When you bring my jacket back, I'll give you a free ride and you can see for yourself.'

'And who should I ask for?' Lizzie said, beginning to enjoy herself. He was gorgeous and the invitation to go on a gondola down the river was exciting. It was almost worth the dip in the smelly river for.

'Ask for Jamie. But I'll not be far away.

I'm working every day.'

'Me too,' she sighed. 'Unless I'm fired for losing all my leaflets. Mr Barrow is a most unforgiving soul.'

On the river bank around them were leaflets that were soaked and muddy from people trampling on them as they had watched her rescue.

His easy grin disappeared to be replaced with a look of concern. 'Do you want me to come with you and I'll explain your accident to this Mr Barrow?'

'Except it wasn't an accident, was it?' Lizzie said grimly. 'Did you see who pushed me?'

He shook his head. 'There was an awful lot of traffic along the river bank. I saw you falling and that you were struggling in the water. Maybe you were shoved or maybe you slipped.'

'I was pushed,' she said, 'I'm sure of that.'

She looked at the river. Her wooden box was floating slowly downstream. Perhaps it was as good a funeral as any for the bird. Like the Vikings that Donald told her stories about.

'Who would want to cause you harm?' Jamie asked. 'Isn't it more likely to have been an elbow by mistake that sent you hurling in?'

She thought about it. Was he right? Had she imagined the sharp thump between her shoulder blades? Could it have simply been the result of the hustle and bustle of too many people on the narrow river bank path? Unbidden, the image of Mr Tunbridge's cold features rose up in her mind. She pushed it down. Ma always told her she had too much imagination.

'Thank you, Jamie. I've got to go.'

'Here, I'll help you gather the leaflets, at least what's left of them. Some of them are all right.'

But most of them were in poor condition and these Lizzie ended up dumping in a litter bin on her way back to the stall. Jamie had been most apologetic even though, as she kept telling him, it wasn't his fault in the slightest.

Despite her wet clothes, she found

herself humming a tune. She was going on a gondola tomorrow. And, she'd see Jamie again. She wondered if he had a sweetheart. Or a wife. Lizzie stopped in her tracks. He was only being kind, offering her a ride in his gondola. She must not read too much into it. Besides, she was hardly a catch. More like a drowned river rat.

Mr Barrow's mood had not improved.

'What took you so long? Did you sell all the tickets?'

'Yes, sir,' she lied with a sweet smile. 'I can even take more out, if you like?'

'No, no, that will do for today.' He frowned at her damp appearance but didn't ask.

She was glad not to have to explain.

★ ★ ★

She went home, expecting to find no-one there. The workers' accommodation was hidden behind fencing and discreet hedging from the rest of the Exhibition. She let herself in to their single, rented room, hearing the sound of Russian voices from next door. In the courtyard, an Indian gymnast practiced bending backwards until her face nearly touched the ground.

'Lizzie, my girl. Why are you back so soon?'

A big bear of a man sat beside the unlit stove. He rubbed a large hand over his stubbled chin. His eyes were tired and pouched. Lizzie noticed the ruddiness on his cheeks and saw the empty brown bottle on the floor.

'Mr Barrow let me away early. Why are you here, Dad? Shouldn't you be over at the Machinery Hall, helping oil the engines?'

'They've let me go, Lizzie lass.' Iain MacDonald's voice was bleak.

'Not again. What's Ma going to say?' Lizzie said in dismay.

Her father's pale blue eyes turned red-rimmed and watery. 'Och, you won't let on, will you?'

Lizzie shook her head. 'You can't keep it from her. She'll find out. What happened this time?'

'Pass me a beer. I need to wet my whistle.'

Lizzie sighed but went to the shelf and took him a bottle. Once he had uncapped it and taken a long, deep suck on it, he burped and patted his belly.

'That's better, lass.'

'Can't you go back to Mr Gorley and tell him you'll do better?' Lizzie said.

'Gorley won't listen to reason. Says I've been late too many mornings.'

Lizzie's chest tightened. Without the pay that her father brought in, what would they do? Ma didn't earn much in the café. Lizzie's work was odd hours, depending on Mr Barrow's whim. Only Donald had a steady job. She sent up a prayer that nothing would change that. They would have to penny pinch even more now. Unless Dad found another job. The trouble was that his reputation was spreading within the community of workers. Many were neighbours and the flimsy housing, made of wood, plaster and painted canvas, meant conversations

31

could easily be heard. It was impossible to keep secrets. Everyone knew everyone else's business. Dad's best friend, Grigory, lived out in rented rooms a tram ride away with some of the other Russians. He passed stories and events in each direction.

'And have you been late?' she asked, knowing the answer already but needing to hear him admit it.

He took another long swig of the bottle. He set it down with a crash.

'You're as bad as your mother with your nagging,' he growled.

'I'm worried, Dad. Ma shouldn't have a job where she has to stand for hours. Her hip is sore. The skin on her hands is broken open from the dish water.'

'What about me? It isn't easy putting food on the table for a wife and three ungrateful children.'

'We are grateful,' Lizzie said. 'But we can't afford to lose work.'

'I should never have left Inverbuie,' Iain mumbled. 'The beautiful heather and the fine blue sea. The pure air in your lungs.'

He stumbled across to the makeshift shelf and grabbed the last bottle. He spoke in Gaelic and Lizzie recognised a lament, as old as the Highland mountains she had grown up beside. Usually the melancholy lilt of it tugged at her heartstrings. Instead, she felt a rising fury for the man who had been turned off the Inverbuie Estate because of his drinking. He had lost their tied cottage and their income and still found pity for himself.

They were lucky to have arrived in Glasgow just as the International Exhibition at Kelvingrove was beginning. There was work to be had. But what about when it finished in November? What were they to do then?

Lizzie's fists clenched. If her father couldn't look after his family, then she was determined to do whatever was necessary to keep them all together.

* * *

Alice let herself in to the townhouse. John, the footman, took her bag and pretended not to notice the disarray of her clothes.

'Is my aunt here?' she asked him.

'Yes, miss. She's in the drawing room. Shall I tell her you will be through, shortly?' His gaze now flickered to her hat and her missing jacket button before he stared straight ahead.

'Thank you,' she said abruptly.

She knew that the story of her odd appearance would spread through the servants as fast as melted butter over toast.

She went upstairs to her bedroom and sank onto the bed. Her head thumped and she really felt as if she could not quite catch her breath. Alice prayed she wasn't going to get sick again. She had been doing so well recently that Mama had not worried about leaving her to visit her cousins in London.

There was a collection of glass vials on her bedside cabinet. Alice rifled through them until she found the dark green bottle of syrup. She took a sip of the sweetened liquid in the hope of feeling more relaxed. The memory of the horror of Mr Tunbridge's grasp on her arm made her shiver. Taking off her jacket and blouse, she saw the imprint of his fingers in red on her upper arm. Mr Tunbridge. She could never think of him as Charles. She felt suddenly nauseous. What kind of man tries to force his fiancé? If that girl Lizzie hadn't come across them, what would have happened?

Unfortunately, she knew what he had intended because he had told her, speaking so closely that she felt his hot breath on her neck.

'I'll ruin you,' he had said, in his clipped voice. As calm and logical as if he was discussing the running of the Exhibition with her father, the facts and figures and income and expenditure that bored her so to hear.

'What do you mean?' she had cried in fear and confusion.

'You'll come with me to the hotel at the far end of the park. I have a suite booked. And there, little Alice, we shall get to know one another.' His eyes bored into hers and she felt as if he was quite mad.

'Please,' she whispered.

'Please?' he mocked. 'You will please me, dear girl. And when I am done, we will be married in haste. I've waited far too long for my son to be born.'

'No, no!' she cried, desperately trying to get away.

He was much stronger than her. She dug in her heels but felt him dragging her towards the shrubbery. Just as her head felt light and she knew she must faint, she saw the girl with her vivid red hair running towards them and shouting.

Dressing now in a fresh skirt and blouse and slipping on a pair of house shoes, Alice thought about Lizzie Mac-Donald. It was truly wonderful that she had come to her rescue. It hardly seemed possible that in such a crowded place, no-one else had seen her struggles. Yet she knew Mr Tunbridge was a powerful and well-known man. After all, he was one of the patrons of the Exhibition. He would have held her closely as he took her to the hotel. If anyone had queried, he would have said she was ill and he was taking her somewhere to rest. She knew this because he had told her so quite calmly.

She took another sip from the green glass bottle before smoothing down her skirts and making her way downstairs. Aunt Hilda rose up from an overstuffed armchair at her arrival.

'Oh, my dear. There you are. You are a little pale today. Was the painting enjoyable? I'm afraid I met Mrs Mellon and dear Miss Christopher and I quite forgot the time. Do sit, dear. Come and sit with me.'

Aunt Hilda's breathy, high-pitched chatter drilled into Alice's painful head. The older woman fussed around her until she was sitting on the sofa opposite, with a soft blanket across her knees and a cushion at her back. Quite as if she was an old lady of fifty, Alice thought with a moment's humour. Of course, having been an invalid for two years, she was used to this. She realised she was tired, and glad of the blanket. Hilda had sent for tea. Soon, the maid had brought a tray. Hilda shooed her away.

'Did you have a lovely time?' she asked, pouring tea into two porcelain cups and offering Alice a small plate of biscuits.

'Mr Tunbridge found me,' Alice said, nibbling at an iced biscuit. Her arm ached and she knew she would have bruises by evening.

Aunt Hilda looked terrified. Her hand went swiftly to her throat to fiddle with the cameo brooch nestled in her ruffled collar.

'Goodness, I should never have left you. Whatever will your Mama say?' Tears welled in her eyes and she mopped them with a lace handkerchief.

'I'm sure she would not say anything,' Alice soothed her.

'My dear, you should have been chaperoned. Never mind your dear mother, what will Mr Tunbridge have thought of you? A young lady of breeding, all alone in that place, surrounded with all sorts of common types.' Hilda shook her head. 'It's all my fault. I was terribly distracted because Mrs Mellon has a wonderful new set of linen she bought at the Exhibition. With pictures of the buildings embroidered onto them. Miss Christopher wanted to see Robertson's coachmakers in one of the halls. She is to be married next spring and requires a new carriage to take her to the church.'

'Is Miss Christopher eager to be wed?' Alice asked. An image of a tall, thin woman with a protruding nose and a favouring for peacock feathers came to her. Aunt Hilda's friend came from a wealthy family and was the last of four sisters to get married.

Hilda looked surprised. 'Of course she is. Doesn't every young lady dream of her wedding?'

'I certainly don't dream of marrying Mr Tunbridge,' Alice said sharply.

Her aunt looked unhappy. 'Your mother, who is my very dear sister … ' she began.

'Mama does not wish it either,' Alice

interrupted her. 'You know that she does not. Won't you speak to Father on my behalf? Tell him that I'm unwell and that I do not wish for Mr Tunbridge to come visiting.'

Aunt Hilda shrank back in her armchair. It seemed she was even more afraid of her brother-in-law than she was of Charles Tunbridge. Alice longed suddenly for her mother. She lived in a house with her father, her aunt and ten servants and yet she felt utterly alone.

'You will feel better soon,' Aunt Hilda said weakly. 'Then you will see much more clearly. You cannot banish your fiancé from visiting the house. What a nonsense. Your father wouldn't hear of such a thing. I don't believe you want that either. Instead, let us talk about your wedding trousseau. I know that your Mama will bring material back from London. What would you like? We can write and tell her.'

It was no use. Aunt Hilda was a kindly but vapid woman who did not like any unpleasantness. This included any kind of disagreement. She was never going to stand up to Alice's father on her behalf.

'Then I shall speak to Father myself,' Alice said, ignoring the attempt to change the conversation and pretending not to see Aunt Hilda's horrified expression.

As it turned out Henry Whittaker was at his office in the shipyards so that Alice had to wait until after dinner before approaching him. She spent the remainder of the afternoon discussing her wedding dress and going away outfits to calm her aunt's nerves.

'I know you and Charles have not yet set a date but a spring wedding is always lovely,' Aunt Hilda chirped, happy now that Alice appeared to be going along with her plans.

When she went to her room, Maggie the housemaid was there.

'Miss Alice, whatever did you do to your lovely hat?' She held up the blue bonnet with its sad-looking ribbons.

'I ... I caught it on a low lying branch,' she said. 'Are you able to mend it for me please?'

'And your jacket?' Maggie said, her eyebrows raised at the lost button.

Alice felt her cheeks flush. She could hardly explain that with a low lying branch. No doubt John, the footman, had spread the story of how she had entered the house in a state of disarray.

'No matter, miss,' Maggie said. 'It'll take me but two seconds to sew a button on.'

'Thank you.'

When Maggie had gone, taking the clothes with her, Alice thought about Lizzie. She had felt bereft when Lizzie had left her in the café. It was as if a light had gone out. The girl had such vitality, so at odds with Alice's fatigue. She intrigued her. Her accent was strange and lilting. It wasn't a working girl's Glasgow accent and certainly wasn't a middle class accent. Besides, she was poorly dressed in a washed out skirt and blouse and with no hat on her bright, red hair. Her boots were dusty and Alice had seen a hole in the leather. She held herself proudly as if she was Alice's equal and hadn't called her Miss Whittaker. Simply Alice.

I'd like to be her friend, she thought. It wasn't possible. They came from different worlds. Alice knew her father was wealthy. She had spent her life surrounded by servants and had always had more than enough to eat, and fashionable clothes to wear. Where did Lizzie live, she wondered. She tried to remember if Lizzie had told her. But she had been dazed with fear from her attack. Had she done all the talking? She recalled Lizzie saying she worked at the Exhibition and that she would find Alice as she was all over the place.

Alice hoped very much that Lizzie would find her. She wanted to find out more about her.

She saw her bag on the floor where John had put it. She opened it and searched through the paintings. There it was. She took the charcoal sketch out and stared at it. Lizzie had caught Alice's likeness in an uncanny way. She had talent. Much more than Alice had. Her watercolours were ordinary. Alice sighed. Then she set her shoulders back. If she had little talent herself, then she could encourage it in someone else. She must see Lizzie again.

Henry Whittaker's library was out of bounds to his wife, sister-in-law and daughter. Maggie was allowed in once a day to dust. So it was with some trepidation that Alice knocked on her father's door after dinner. He had not dined with them, having gone to his club. Aunt Hilda had kept up a warbling conversation which Alice had only half concentrated upon. Enough to supply answers which satisfied her aunt.

Now, she stood outside the library on the second floor of the townhouse and waited, her heart beating painfully in her chest.

'Come,' Henry barked from the interior.

Alice took a deep, reviving breath and stepped inside. It was a dark-panelled room, smelling of wood polish and cigars. Bookcases covered the walls, filled with hundreds of leather-bound books on all sorts of topics. Her father sat in his large, walnut chair behind his study table, an open ledger before him and a glass of whiskey at its side. A cigar loosened a curl of grey smoke from a dish beside the glass. The smoke rose lazily into the still air.

'Father,' she said, nervously.

'Alice. Did I call for you?' Henry frowned.

His eyes fixed back on the ledger with its spidery black ink columns of figures and notes. He was making it plain that she had interrupted him in his important work. He didn't need to spell it out. She was always in the way. Alice wanted to tell him he should be grateful he had a child. She was the only surviving offspring out of five pregnancies that her mother had endured. It wasn't her fault she wasn't a boy. If Henry had been a different sort of father, she might have learned about the ship building industry and been a help to him. However, as it was, she was simply a mouth to feed and a vague annoyance. When he remembered her, which wasn't often.

'No, you didn't,' she said, moistening her lips.

'Has your mother written?' He looked at her then.

'I received a letter yesterday. She is well and enjoying London. She sent her regards and there is a letter in the post to you.'

Her father made a satisfied sound in his throat. He turned a page of the ledger. She waited until he looked up as if surprised to see her still standing there.

'That's not why I came to speak to you,' she said.

'What is it then?'

A log shifted in the fireplace with a crackling noise. Below, she heard Aunt Hilda talking to someone, probably Mrs Kearns, the housekeeper. Outside the window, it was not yet dusk. It was the middle of summer and dusk came late at ten pm just as the Exhibition shut for the day. Across the street, if she was able to walk across to the glass and peer out, she would see the Grand Electric Illuminations which transformed the Exhibition nightly into a fairyland of coloured lights. They were turned on whether it was dark or not so that the visitors could be impressed.

'It's about Mr Tunbridge,' Alice said.

'I do wish you would call him Charles. He has asked you to, several times, and I have given you permission to do so,' Henry said testily.

'Charles, then,' she said quickly.

'What about him? Hurry up, girl. I have work to do this evening. Your aunt is here to keep you company.'

'I don't want to marry him.' The words echoed in the stuffy room. The mixture of wood smoke, cigar smoke and whiskey fumes made her light-headed. Or maybe it was her boldness in speaking the truth.

Her father stared at her, as if his whiskey glass had found its voice and broken into song. Then colour began to rise in his face, seeping up from his bushy beard until it reached his spectacles. Alice took a step back. He had not invited her to sit, and her legs felt weak and shaky. She tried to imagine Lizzie standing beside her. She couldn't imagine her being afraid.

'It is not your business,' he said. 'Charles is an old friend of mine. He needs a wife and you must be married. You will be well looked after and have status in society. He has connections to the royalty.'

I don't care, she wanted to scream. I hate him and I'd rather be poor and homeless than marry a monster. But she daren't say that.

'You are a very ungrateful young woman. I have clothed you and fed you for eighteen long years. Now you have the opportunity to better yourself and be a credit to your Mama and I and instead you say you do not want to marry. I do not believe it. Has your aunt put you up to this?'

'No, Aunt Hilda has nothing to do with it,' Alice said, annoyed he thought she had no ideas for herself.

'I won't hear another word on the

subject. You will marry Charles and that is that.'

'Mama doesn't want me to marry until I have good health.'

'You are much improved, are you not? It's been two years since your illness.'

'You look healthy to me,' Henry said, firmly. 'Do not use it as an excuse. Your mother thinks as I do.'

Mama might wheedle or gently persuade and in matters of the household she usually won her way. In the matter of the convenient and advantageous marriage of his only daughter, she would not win against Henry's ambitions. The Whittakers were wealthy but it was new money. The Tunbridges had both money and old connections. Alice's sacrifice was a pathway glittering with potential for her father.

'In fact,' her father said now, 'especially after this little chat, I think it's time to set a date for the wedding. I will write to your mother. The Exhibition will end on the ninth of November. After that, Charles will be less busy. A December wedding will suit very nicely. Go down-stairs and please inform your aunt.'

He turned away from her and she was dismissed. Stung, Alice walked out of the study, letting the door slam behind her. She had only made it worse. Instead of being free, she now had a wedding date only four months hence. She stood in the hallway. Then a tiny smile curved her lips. There was still hope. For Alice had a secret. A secret she nursed and which might save her yet.

3

Lizzie loved the evening best. Even before it was dusk, the Grand Electric Illuminations would go on, lighting up the Exhibition grounds with colours which gleamed against the darkening sky. It gave the park a special magic and set the visitors to chattering with awe. She liked to slip away and walk the pathways. The crowds were a little less thick than during the day. The school groups had vanished, the young children and families too. Now, it was mainly couples that strolled, listening to the music or going to the theatre or the great concert hall.

She didn't have the money to pay for a ticket to the shows but was content to watch other people laughing as they went in or out. She saw the showmen and acrobats practicing daily and so felt she had seen the shows anyway. Many of the coffee houses and restaurants were still open and doing a raging trade.

Even better were the hours after ten o'clock when the Exhibition finally shut for the day. Then it belonged to the people who worked there. Tired stall holders shutting up shop, exhausted performers taking the last tram home or heading for the temporary housing where the MacDonalds lived. There were a few quiet night hours before it all started up once more in preparation for the daily opening at nine-thirty.

She headed for Mrs Morgan's coffee shop. Mrs Morgan had pulled down the shutters and turned the lights low to indicate she was closed. She smiled at Lizzie.

'Come for your mother? She's mopping the back room floor. On you go. Mind you don't slip.'

Mary put the mop aside when she saw Lizzie. 'Let's go home. My hip's aching and I need to sit down.'

'I'll make the supper,' Lizzie said, giving her mother the crook of her arm to steady her.

She hesitated. Mary looked at her hard.

'What is it? What's wrong? Is it Iona? I sent her home a while back to peel the tatties.'

'She's peeled them and got the water boiling.'

'Then what's the matter?'

'Oh, Ma, I don't know how to tell you this … ' Lizzie began, reluctantly.

'No, no.' Mary's eyes widened in realisation. 'Tell me it isn't true. He promised he'd keep this job.'

Lizzie could hardly meet her gaze, seeing the disappointment and fear there. Mary's fingers clutched at her arm. They were nearly at the compound before her mother spoke again quietly.

'He's still your father. He's head of the household and we give him our respect. He'll find something else. He always does.'

'It's us who keep it together, Ma,' Lizzie said fiercely, 'You, me and Donald. Even Iona helps by working with you and helping at home. Him, he does a wee bit here and a wee bit there until they kick him off for the drinking.'

Mary hushed her as they went in to the makeshift room. Lizzie bit her lip and tasted blood. She balled her hands, wanting to hit out and scream with frustration. Iain sat where she'd left him. The beer was long gone. He stank of it, and stale sweat. Mary went to him and kissed his brow.

'It's alright,' she murmured.

'Och, Mary, my love. It's that Gorley. He's a devil. Always on at me. I did nothing wrong. But don't you worry, my sweet. First thing tomorrow, I'll be out getting work.'

'Lizzie, help Iona put the dinner out,' Mary said firmly. 'Donald, lay the cutlery and cups.' She sat with her husband, holding his hand, and avoiding her children's concerned glances.

Donald, a much slimmer and younger version of Iain, stretched his long legs and with good humour went to set the small table. He whispered to Lizzie as she stirred the stew.

'Haven't we been here before? Cheer up, sister mine. We'll get by.'

The meal was a silent one for a little while. Nothing but the clink of cups and spoons and the scrape of a chair leg on the stone floor. Iain looked downcast. Probably sad that there was no more beer, Lizzie thought bitterly. Mary fussed over him, giving him the largest portion of stew and making sure he got the meat chunks. The rest of the plates were more cabbage and potatoes than meat. Iona kicked at her chair legs until Donald told her to stop. He ate heartily, never one to let worries get in the way of his hunger. Lizzie picked at her plate, her appetite gone.

'Did you bury your bird?' Mary asked, breaking the awkward mood.

Lizzie put down her spoon. 'It had a river burial in the end. But I had a strange experience.' She described what had happened. She left out how threatening Alice's attacker had seemed, and made out as if she had slipped into the river by accident. Her story focussed more on

Alice and her fascination with, and pity for, such a rich, young lady. When she had finished they were all smiling at her.

'What?' she said with a puzzled shrug.

'It's Lizzie MacDonald to the rescue,' Donald teased. 'This poor Alice hasn't got a chance.'

'I wish I'd seen her,' Iona breathed, 'I'd like to see her blue hat and her rich clothes.'

'You be careful, Lizzie,' Mary said. 'You're too tender with creatures that need help. You don't know this Alice at all. And she's a different class altogether. The toffs aren't like us.'

'She's very nice,' Lizzie protested. 'She gave me paper to sketch on and said I had real talent. But I did feel sorry for her. She came across as so lonely. I probably won't see her again, but if I do, I'll talk to her.'

Donald snorted. 'Lonely. I bet she has an army of servants in her grand home to keep her company. Ma's right, watch yourself. People like that, they use you and spit you out after.'

'As for this Jamie who's offered you a gondola ride, you can go but mind your manners and don't let him take advantage of you. Don't give the gossips fuel. Mrs Morgan will be first to hear of any goings on,' Mary warned.

'It's only a boat ride along the river,' Lizzie protested. 'It'll take all of half an hour and that'll be the end of it. Hardly enough minutes for him to ravish me.'

'Honestly, that's enough,' Mary said, in her tone of voice that brooked no more argument. Donald risked a grin and a wink at Lizzie, while Iona giggled until she was told to leave the table. Iain sighed and rubbed at his mouth, a lingering glance at the empty bottles making him swallow.

'Say, son, can I come and work on your stall?' he asked.

Donald worked on a stall selling souvenir plates. There were earthenware plates and, for a higher price, porcelain plates. Donald painted each with a scene of the Groveries and a title: 'A Present from Glasgow'

He shook his head. 'Sorry, Dad. There's only room for Harry and myself. If he had to pay you as well, he wouldn't get his profit.' Harry rented the stall and bought the plates and tools. Donald could have added that his skills required a steady hand. Iain's hands shook visibly and he staggered as he launched himself up for an evening smoke.

★ ★ ★

The next day, Lizzie hurried to sell her tickets so that she could go to the river and find Jamie. Her voice trilled and tempted the customers with news of the day's shows and music entertainments until with satisfaction she saw the tickets and leaflets had all gone. Mr Barrow was not to know that she had sold and distributed them in an hour and not a whole morning. She would go and collect more at lunch time from him. In the meantime, she had a couple of hours of freedom which she meant to make the most of.

It was a warm, breezy day and she was

wearing her green skirt, mercifully dried. She had put it beneath the mattress at night to flatten out the creases. Her blouse was clean and she had borrowed a straw bonnet from Ma. Not that she was out to impress Jamie, she told herself firmly. She just wanted to look good. That was all. She couldn't help being pleased that the bonnet's ties matched her skirt. Ma had found a length of ribbon she'd bought from the travelling tinker last winter. Back in Inverbuie. She drew in a breath, and refused to feel sad on such a fine day.

Down at the jetty on the river, two gondoliers lounged in the sun. Four gondolas were underway, filled with happy customers pointing at the ducks and exclaiming at the views of the Groveries as they floated past. The gondoliers were singing in rich, melodic Italian. Lizzie grinned happily and almost skipped to the jetty.

'Ah, bella donna,' the shorter of the two gondoliers purred as she arrived. 'You wish to travel as if you are in my beautiful Venice? To take an authentic gondola and I will sing you an Aria to make you weep with joy.'

'Hush, Freddy.' Jamie grinned. 'This is Lizzie I was telling you about. The girl I saved from the river yesterday.'

Freddy, short and dark, squinted in the sunlight at Lizzie. 'My friend, you did not lie. She is indeed very pretty.'

Jamie said quickly, 'Don't mind Freddy. He has a talent for the dramatic. Have you come for that trip on the river?'

Lizzie felt warm inside. Had Jamie really said she was pretty? No-one had ever told her that before. Mary wasn't one for compliments except to say if someone was kind or good at heart. Her Dad was too busy fighting life to think of such things. As for Donald and Iona, they would sooner throw her back in the river than tell her she was bonny.

'Frederico Bianchi at your service, Miss Lizzie.'

Freddy bowed low before her before straightening up. He was the same height as her and Jamie towered over them both.

'You did promise me a boat ride,' she said to Jamie, worried he had forgotten. 'Free,' she added. She had no money to pay.

Jamie laughed. 'Free, it is. Freddy's worried now he won't get paid. But you'll get your cash, Freddy, I promise because I'll pay it myself. Now, Lizzie, if you step this way and mind your boots on the uneven surface of the jetty. We can't have you falling in again.'

She took his offered hand, feeling the callouses and the strength of it. Her fingers tingled where they touched him and she wondered if he felt it too. All of a sudden shy, she dipped her gaze and concentrated on placing her feet carefully into the gondola. It swayed under her weight and she sat down on the wooden seat. Now the water, green and thick, was so close. She pushed away memories of it from the day before. She was safe with Jamie. She felt it.

He got in too and took a long pole to

punt them along. Freddy waved a lazy goodbye. More people had reached the jetty and he turned to talk to them. Lizzie heard his Italian phrases as he charmed them.

'Do you want a song?' Jamie asked as the gondola moved along the river. 'That's included in the price, you know.'

'Except I haven't paid.'

'You get the full service. This is my treat.'

'Maybe I'll have a song later.' Lizzie smiled. 'For now, I'd like to enjoy being on the water and pretending I'm in Venice. Isn't that where Freddy said he was from?'

'I'm fairly certain he's from Rome.' Jamie grinned. 'The nearest he's been to Venice is probably touching a postcard picture of it.'

'Oh, well, it's all magical here, myths and made up dreams,' Lizzie sighed.

'Is that a good thing?'

'That depends on who's dreaming. If you take my Dad, it's bad. He dreams of his home in the Highlands and can't accept the reality that we're here in Glasgow to stay. He hates the grime and the bustle. Too many folks for him. And, he's lost his job.' The words were out of her mouth before she filtered them. 'I'm sorry, you don't want to hear my troubles.'

'I don't mind. I'm sorry he's lost his work. That's hard. Is he any good with boats? Freddy could use some help with maintaining the gondolas.'

'He's lately worked in the Machinery Hall, oiling engines and keeping them going. So, he'd manage the boats alright.' Lizzie couldn't tell him about the drinking. She didn't know him well enough. She could only pray that Dad wouldn't mess this opportunity up.

'I'll have a word with Freddy.'

'You don't have to,' she said, embarrassed.

'It's no bother,' he said easily.

They floated along slowly. The sun heated her skin and she was glad of the straw bonnet.

'The water doesn't smell too good.'

She made a face.

'Aye, you're right there. The ladies usually hold their hankies to their noses while the men smoke cigars to mask the stink.'

'I don't have a hanky so I'll have to put up with it.'

'At least you're not in the water today,' he grinned.

'Did I thank you for saving me? Because I meant to. Only I was distracted.'

'Thanks accepted.'

He brought the gondola to a stop under a large willow tree whose trailing leaves brushed the water and gave some shade to the river bank.

'We'll rest here a moment then I'll punt us back to the jetty.'

There was a silence between them but it wasn't unpleasant. Jamie sat at the far end of the gondola from Lizzie and she felt confused. If he'd asked for a kiss, she might have given him one. But there was no sign that he was after that. Maybe she had read him wrong. He didn't fancy her in the slightest and was only being polite.

To break it, and her thoughts, she asked him, 'Do you know a Mr Tunbridge?'

'I know of him. Why?'

She told him what had happened with Alice and how her attacker turned out to be her fiancé.

Jamie's eyebrows raised as she finished. 'And you think this same man pushed you into the river?'

Lizzie shook her head. 'I don't know. Maybe it was an accident. It was busy on the footpath.'

Jamie looked serious. 'Mr Tunbridge is an important man. He's a patron of the Exhibition and a personal friend of James Paton who is the Superintendent of Museums.'

'How do you know that?' Lizzie frowned. Jamie was only a gondolier, he wasn't gentry, so how could he know their business?

'Freddy talks a lot. He attends the Exhibition management meetings and Mr Tunbridge goes to those. Freddy owns the gondolas, you see.'

Lizzie's look of surprise made him chuckle.

'Freddy's a modest chap. You wouldn't know he's the owner from talking to him.'

'And what does he have to say about Mr Tunbridge?' Lizzie asked, pulling at the willow leaves.

'He says he's wealthy and powerful and not the sort to make an enemy of.'

A shiver ran down her spine. The leaves turned to mush in her palm, leaving green streaks. She flung them over the side of the gondola and wiped her fingers on her skirt.

'Can we go back now, please?'

'Are you alright?' Jamie asked. 'You've no reason to be afraid of him. He lives in very different circles from you or me. You're no threat to him. In fact, I'd wager he's forgotten all about you by now.'

Lizzie saw that he wasn't taking her seriously. Which was fair enough. He didn't know her well. And he hadn't seen the expression on Charles Tunbridge's face when he pushed past her, leaving

Alice on the ground.

'Maybe you're right. I'm ready to go back now,' she said again.

Jamie shrugged and turned the gondola around expertly. They didn't speak as they returned to the jetty. He jumped off first and then gave her his hand to pull her onto the wooden platform. There was a small queue with people impatiently waving tickets. The family in front pushed forward without waiting. Lizzie had to nod her thanks at Jamie. He looked as if he wanted to say something but what more was there to say, she thought. He didn't believe her. She watched as the gondola swung out into the river again. Jamie's broad shoulders flexed as he wielded the punt. The sun glinted on his dark brown hair. She felt the instant flicker of attraction. Just as she turned to leave, he whistled. She looked back.

'See you tomorrow?' he shouted.

Lizzie's heart soared. She waved and grinned, before practically skipping back to Mr Barrow for her next batch of tickets.

Harry had a prime spot for his stall, not far from the Palace of Industry and not far from Miss Cranston's Tea Rooms which were the most popular venue to take refreshments in the whole of the Exhibition. He was an older man with craggy features and a gruff persona which hid a kind heart. Donald had liked him immediately. He had taken a chance on hiring Donald without casting a comment on him being new to Glasgow. Harry was himself an outsider, having come up from London to try his luck.

The rules did not allow anything to be sold that was not made in the Exhibition itself. Harry, like other wily vendors, got round this by buying plain plates and then having them illustrated on site. Donald's job was to paint the plates.

The best part of his job was Harry's daughter, Anna. She brought the batches of plates and often helped with the decorating of them. She didn't speak to Donald more than she could help. Which was a pity, he thought now, stealing a glance at her dipped head. She wasn't pretty in the traditional sense. Her nose was too long, her lips too wide. But she had thick, corn-blond hair and a sprinkling of freckles over her cheekbones that he found appealing. She was a challenge, too. He was annoyed that she appeared to despise him.

Donald had left a sweetheart at home. He had fully expected to marry her until the MacDonalds had been thrown off Inverbuie and told not to return. His girl had closed the door on him when he went to beg her to leave with him. He was still hurting from the fact she hadn't loved him enough. He had imagined himself in love with her. Now, he realised he could find other girls attractive. If Anna would be nice to him, he could easily fall in love with her.

She stretched and he tried not to notice how her blouse moulded to her chest with the movement. A single curl escaped her bun and he longed to tuck it behind her neat, little ear.

'Have you finished those?' Anna said, pointing at the stack of plates beside him.

'I've done ten,' he said.

'I'll put them on display.'

They were sitting at the back of the stall, with the paints and other paraphernalia. At the front was a display shelf. Anna took the plates and set them out. Harry was doing a good trade. He had the knack of a salesman, calling out to passers-by, enticing them to buy a souvenir.

'What about a present from Glasgow?' he called to one well-dressed woman with a small girl clinging to her skirts. 'A souvenir from the greatest exhibition this new century. None bigger than this right 'ere. Most of the world has come visiting this great city. Look at this plate, madam. A lovely picture of the Palace of Industry by my talented artists. Will you buy?'

Donald smiled as the woman did indeed buy a plate. Anna looked sour. She sat back beside him with a sigh.

'Pass me that brush. Father will want another batch of ten before lunch, by the looks of it.'

'He's good at selling.'

She made a disparaging sound.

'Why are you grumpy?' he said, irritated. He should have been used to her moods by now but it grated. 'You should be glad. It's food on your table.'

He thought about his own father and how useless he was. Iain had been left at home this morning, whining after Ma that it wasn't his fault he had no job.

'Never you mind,' Anna said rudely.

Donald shrugged. 'Suit yourself.'

She was none of his business. He decided he didn't fancy her after all. She was far too much effort, and a real sourpuss. He picked up his paint brush and took a new porcelain plate. This was finer work than the cheaper earthenware and needed real concentration. His vision blurred briefly. He blinked and it cleared. He thought no more about it.

4

Several days had passed since Alice's conversation with her father in his study. She had spent them in bed, feeling faint and sick. The room smelt of Ayers Cherry Pectoral tonic and her own unwashed body and hair. She had insisted that the curtains remain closed and the lamps unlit as they pained her eyes. Aunt Hilda had fussed around her.

'I'll send up a little supper,' she had said on the first evening, shortly after Alice had stormed out of her father's study and gone to her bedroom. Alice had called for Maggie's help to remove her corset and then got into bed and pulled the sheets and coverlet up to her chin. She had fallen asleep after the supper of milk posset and hot chocolate. When the morning came, she felt unwell and stayed in bed.

'Oh, my dear, whatever is the matter?' Aunt Hilda said, after Maggie had informed her that Miss Alice was ill. 'I do hope this isn't the start of all your troubles once more. Perhaps I should write to your dear Mama and beg her to come home?'

'No, you mustn't do that. Promise me,' Alice said, sitting up in bed in agitation.

Aunt Hilda plumped up the pillows behind Alice's head and looked distressed. 'Well, if you're sure you won't be an invalid, then I won't write. Only, I can't bear the idea of you in bed for months the way it was before. I visited regularly, as you will remember, and let your poor Mama have some time away from your bedside. It was exhausting for all of us.'

'Quite,' Alice said sharply, before sinking slowly back onto the bed with a sigh. 'I don't feel well, it's true but I won't have Mama worried about me. I'm sure I will be up and about in a few days.'

'A few days,' Aunt Hilda wailed. 'So long?'

'So long,' Alice said, her lips pursed with determination. 'But it could be longer if you keep fussing over me. Really, I will be fine. I just need peace and quiet. If Mr Tunbridge asks to visit, I hope you will tell him I am unwell and unable to receive him.'

Aunt Hilda's hands instinctively went to her brooch as if it could protect her from mention of his name.

'And Father too,' Alice added, 'I don't want to see him.'

'Why ever not?' her aunt asked in surprise. 'Has he upset you?'

Alice shook her head and wouldn't say. Maybe if she didn't voice what her father had dictated, she could pretend it hadn't happened. The thought of marrying Mr Tunbridge in four months' time was too horrific to dwell on. Which is why being in bed and hiding under the covers was a way of blanking it all out. She truly did feel ill, she told herself. She wasn't imagining it.

Aunt Hilda paced the room, picking up ornaments and putting them down again, twitching the curtains into place and moving an occasional table that got in her way until Alice wanted to scream. Eventually she suggested that her aunt go downstairs and enjoy her embroidery and send Maggie up to sit with her. Aunt Hilda wrung her hands while she considered this. Finally, she agreed, on the condition that Alice call her the minute she felt worse.

When Maggie appeared, Alice told her she could have the rest of the evening for herself as long as she didn't tell her aunt or Alice's father. With a happy Maggie gone upstairs to the servants' quarters, Alice slid down in the bed with a contented sigh. A few days in bed and she would be well enough to face the world. She hoped by then her father might have reconsidered his words.

This morning, she felt as if she had more energy. She called Maggie and asked for a jug of hot water to be brought to her bedroom. She washed her hair and body, feeling refreshed afterwards. Once dried, she called the maid again to help her dress. Maggie then opened the curtains to let the bright daylight flood the room.

'Where is my father?' Alice asked.

'He's in the breakfast room, Miss. Shall I tell him you're joining him? Mrs Brown is there too.'

'Yes, please do. Let Aunt Hilda and Father know I will be with them shortly. Thank you, Maggie.'

It was a good half hour later before Alice descended the main staircase. She had dressed in her favourite dress, a navy blue velvet creation with becoming white lace at the neckline and the cuffs. Her new cream kid boots felt soft and smart as she heard the heels click on the tiled floor of the entrance hallway. John, the footman, gave her a small bow as she passed but she ignored him. She didn't trust him one inch. She was certain he told her father all that went on amongst the household.

The breakfast room had an enormous bow window that looked out across the road to the parkland and Groveries in the distance. A walnut sideboard was covered in silver breakfast dish tureens. Alice smelt scrambled eggs, toasted bread and kippers and found that her appetite had recovered. Her father and aunt were sitting together at a long table with their backs to the fine view.

Her father stood up as she came in. He mopped at his moustaches with a napkin.

'My dear, it's good to see you. Are you well?'

'I am much better, thank you, Father.'

'There are eggs and ham and fish. Will you have a little of each?' Aunt Hilda said. 'I can ring for the maid to serve you. The kippers are delicious and I can get the girl to fetch more toast. Why only yesterday … '

As she chattered on, Alice zoned her out while smiling and nodding. What she really wanted, was to go with her father that morning to his work. She waited until she was sitting at the table with them, a plate of scrambled eggs and toast in front of her and a small cup of coffee wafting fragrant steam, to her side.

Her father was nervous. He tapped on the table, began to light his pipe and left it and then coughed twice. He glanced sideways at Alice when he thought she wasn't watching. Alice smiled inwardly. He didn't like it when she was sick. She hoped he was regretting his harsh words to her.

'Are you going to your shipyards this morning?' she asked.

'I am indeed, my dear.'

'I would so love to accompany you, Father. If I may?'

'Are you well enough to leave the house today?' Henry said.

'I feel much better. Fresh air is what I need.'

'Very well. Usually I am too busy but today you may come with me. I have a full day's work ahead of me but Taylor can bring you back in the carriage. That is, if your aunt agrees?'

Hilda's mouth dropped open in amazement until she remembered her manners and closed it. Her sister's husband never asked for her opinion. She was flustered now she had to make a decision. She nodded and nodded.

'If Alice feels up to it then some fresh air will do her good, I imagine. Don't tire yourself out, dear.'

'Very well, your aunt believes it will do you good. Be ready to leave in twenty minutes.' Henry stood up, picked up his unlit pipe and left the room.

There was a small silence during which Alice finished her eggs happily and Hilda drank her tea and her eyebrows nearly met the frilly edge of her cap.

'Goodness, he hardly speaks to me and then asks what I think. Whatever brought that on?'

'He's concerned about my health and he doesn't want to take the full responsibility if I collapse during a visit to the shipyards,' Alice said. 'Mama would never forgive him.'

'Alice, really. He's concerned about you and merely wishes you healthy. I doubt the rest of what you have said. Now, go and get ready. Your father won't wait for you.'

But today, he would wait, Alice knew. He would not want a return to two years before when she had had pneumonia which lingered. None of them did.

The Whittakers' carriage took them along streets busy with other carriages, carts and horses and trams. Pedestrians dashed between the vehicles and Alice's impression was of top hats and flat caps, ladies' parasols and beribboned hats. The buildings were black with soot and the smell of horses' dung, coal, fish and vegetables stung her nostrils as they passed by the shops with their striped awnings. They drove over the iron bridge on the River Clyde and soon were in Govan. This area of Glasgow was where the main shipyards were to be found. As far as her eyes could see, there were masts and scaffolds and glimpses of huge ocean liners, steamers and navy vessels under construction.

'This is the power house of the Empire,' Henry said proudly, following her gaze. 'At least a quarter of all ships on the sea today are built on Clydeside.'

'Goodness,' Alice said politely. She was not at all interested but knew that her father took great pride in his work as a manager at the Tunbridge Ship Building and Engineering Offices. She also knew she didn't have to be afraid of seeing Charles that day as Aunt Hilda had told her he was busy at the Exhibition every day that week.

'Now, my dear, I must leave you,' Henry said, once they were inside the offices, which faced directly on to the street. The dark wood panelled entrance hall was very impressive and busy with men walking swiftly to and from their tasks. He frowned. 'What do you wish to do?'

'I remembered last time I came with you, there was a young man called William Morrow who told me fascinating tales of the ships being built. I was intrigued.'

Henry's expression lightened. Alice pretended to look eager. Her father had no son to share his enthusiasm for ships with so he was easy to fool into believing she had an interest. She did have an interest here, but not for the ships.

'I'll send William down. He can spare a half hour. No longer. Then you must take the carriage home. I have to attend a board meeting now.'

Alice waited happily in the entrance hall, sitting with her skirts daintily tucked in so that her new boots could be glimpsed. She didn't have to wait for long. Soon, a tall, thin young man with sandy hair and warm hazel eyes approached her with a smile.

'William! How lovely to see you.'

'Miss Whittaker, the pleasure is all mine. Your father has asked me to accompany you on a small tour of the yard and to inform you about the ship building we are undertaking.'

Alice stifled the urge to roll her eyes. Sometimes men could be quite obtuse. She didn't care one whit about the ships. She did care about William. She had met him a few weeks ago and been escorted around by him while her father had a meeting. Since then, she had thought of him often. He had a handsome face with a long nose and blunt jaw and she liked the broadness of his shoulders. He had seemed keen on her too. Now she wondered if she had imagined it. Until she looked up at him and saw the warmth of his gaze.

She smiled. 'I would love a walk around.'

'Would you like to see what I'm working on?'

William was a junior draughtsman and she knew he worked in the offices on the first floor which were full of draughtsmen and engineers poring over large technical drawings which made no sense to her.

'Maybe later. Right now, I'd love some fresh air. I've been rather unwell.'

'I'm sorry to hear that.' His face creased in concern, and Alice wanted to stroke the furrow of his brow where it met the bridge of his nose.

'I'm much better now that I've seen you,' she whispered.

William glanced around nervously. He took her arm and pulled her down a side hallway which was quiet.

'Alice — Miss Whittaker, you mustn't speak so. You are engaged to the owner of this very shipyard. My employer.'

'You gave me a poem,' she said simply.

William flushed. 'I shouldn't have done so.'

'Why did you then?'

'Because — '

'It was a lovely poem,' Alice said, 'I've read it and read it. I can't believe you wrote it yourself.'

He looked pleased then worried again.

'I can't stop thinking about you,' Alice went on. 'Have you thought at all about me?'

He groaned and shook his head. 'I have thought about you but I must not.'

'Don't say that, William. I'd rather hear you say that you have another beautiful poem just for me.'

He fumbled in his jacket pocket and pulled out a sheaf of small papers.

Alice gasped. 'Are these all poems?'

William nodded. 'You are very inspiring. After we met, I couldn't stop writing.'

He took the top sheet and gave it to

her. Alice clasped it to her chest dramat-
ically.

'I'll read it later. When I'm alone.
Thank you.'

'I — I find you very attractive. Even if
it's wrong.'

'It's not wrong. I feel the same about
you,' Alice said, feeling a tide of happiness wash over her. She was so used to
feeling scared and anxious about her
engagement, she had forgotten what
happiness was. 'What are we going to
do?'

'Do?' William glanced around but there
was no-one there. 'What can we do?'

'We must think of something,' Alice
cried, tears glistening and threatening to
fall. 'I can't bear it otherwise.'

'You must bear it,' he said hurriedly.
'We can pass letters to each other. And
you can visit here.'

'My father won't often bring me.'
There was a silence while they both con-
templated their situation. Then Alice
had an idea. 'Can you visit the Exhibition? I'm often there alone, painting.

My aunt is easily distracted. Please, say you'll come?'

William nodded. 'I work long hours here but I have a half day on a Wednesday and I don't work on Sundays.'

'It's very busy in the Groveries, but I'm often down beside the river with my easel and paints.'

'I'll find you,' he promised.

Alice went home in the carriage, the piece of paper burning a hole in her pocket. She would read it in the safety of her bedroom. William liked her too. He had told her so. Now all she had to do was keep her secret safe, until she worked out what to do. She deliberately thought no further than enjoying the anticipation of the poem. She savoured it. Because beyond that, she had no clue what to do about her engagement and how to escape it.

★ ★ ★

Lizzie and her father walked across from their rooms to the river with Iona skipping along behind them. Mary had finally given in to her pleas to be allowed to go with them and see the gondolas. This was on strict instructions that she was not to go near the river in case she fell in just like Lizzie had.

'You can't swim neither,' her mother said, brushing Iona's thick, brown hair and lacing a red ribbon into it. 'There, at least you look respectable. Now, where are you to go after seeing the boats?'

'I'm to come straight back to Mrs Morgan's and help dry the dishes,' Iona said obediently, but her dark eyes flashed with excitement and Lizzie was certain she wasn't listening to Ma, not really.

'And you're not to bother Dad or Lizzie. It's important that your Dad gets this job.' Mary bit her lip, and her fingers, gently lying on Iona's thin shoulders, tightened involuntarily.

'Ma, you're hurting me,' Iona whined, wriggling free.

'Sorry, my darling. I didn't mean to. Here, give me a kiss before you go.'

Iona flung herself into Ma's arms and

kissed her cheek. 'I'll tell you all about the boats when I get back.'

'You do that,' Mary smiled at her youngest child.

Iain had washed and shaved his face. Lizzie thought he looked reasonable apart from the red-rimmed eyelids and heavy pouches under his eyes. Never mind, he'd have to do. He cast a last fond glance at the beer bottles and kissed his wife on her lips before shambling out of the room. Mary frowned after him and grabbed Lizzie's arm as she made to follow him out.

'He has to get this job. You make sure of it. Promise me?'

'I'll try. Freddy seems like a good sort and Dad has the skills to mend the gondolas. As long as he — '

'He has to keep it this time,' Mary said, cutting in, her normally gentle tone now fierce. 'This is his last chance. People know him only too well. Who else will offer him labour?'

Lizzie didn't answer. There was no need. She hurried after her father and sent up a quick prayer that all would be well.

The day was overcast but that hadn't stopped the crowds swelling. A brass band was playing, its loud notes making the air vibrate around them. A football match was starting over in the brand new stadium and she heard the shrill whistle and the roar of the onlookers in the distance. It was a full house and she had sold every ticket Mr Barrow had given her for it. With the lack of a sunny day, there were less people inclined to punt down the river. When they reached the jetty, there was no queue at all. A few of the gondolas were out, slowly winding downstream and the willows quivered in the breeze.

Freddy came out of a wooden shed not far from the jetty and waved them over. Beside her, Lizzie heard her father swallow. Iona was gathering pebbles beside the path.

'Stay here,' Lizzie warned. 'Don't go near the river.'

Iona nodded vaguely and continued

to sort her stones into different colours and sizes.

'Ah, bella Lizzie, and this must be your esteemed father,' Freddy smiled, his arm outstretched in greeting.

Looking somewhat bemused by the Italian's flamboyance, Iain shook the offered hand.

'You're looking for employment, yes?' Freddy said, beckoning them over to the shed.

Iain brushed his knuckles to his mouth. 'I am, indeed, sir. I've got all the skills and experience you need to mend the boats. I surely do.'

Lizzie winced inwardly. Her father sounded needy. But when she dared to look up again, Freddy was throwing her a warm glance. She realised that Jamie must have told him everything. Torn between annoyance that he had done so and relief that she didn't have to explain or defend her Dad, Lizzie stumbled after them into the low light of the shed.

Jamie was there, lifting sacks onto shelves. He turned as they came in and winked at Lizzie. She felt a flush rise in her cheeks and was thankful no-one could notice in the shadows.

'This is Jamie, he rescued me from the river,' she said to her father.

'Thanks are not enough,' Iain said. 'You have my eternal gratitude for saving Lizzie.'

'I was in the right place at the right moment. But she'd have got out by herself if I hadn't been.'

'You're too modest, mio amico.' Freddy clapped him on the back, heartily. 'Anyway, here is Mr MacDonald, who is going to maintain the gondolas for us. Will you show him what has to be done?'

'I've got the job?' Iain asked in amazement. 'But I haven't told you what experience I've got of looking after machines and — '

Freddy waved his hand in kind dismissal. 'Not necessary, Mr MacDonald. You're Lizzie's father and Jamie says you need the work.'

'Yes, sir. I do need the work. I had to

leave — ' He didn't finish what he was saying.

Lizzie squirmed and begged him silently not to explain why he had no job. Iain gave a deep sigh and stood still, his shoulders sagging.

'Well, that's all sorted.' Freddy grinned. 'I have to get back to singing for the ladies as we sail down the beautiful river. Please forgive me.'

He went off whistling a tune that Lizzie didn't recognise but thought was lovely.

'Funny fellow,' her father murmured to her.

'Freddy owns all this, Dad,' she said quietly, 'So, you'll need to keep on his good side, if you see what I'm saying?'

'I promised your Ma, and I'm promising you now, lass. This time it'll be alright.'

Lizzie didn't answer. She let Jamie take him to the boats stored in the shed and before they noticed she had slipped away. After all, Mr Barrow was waiting with that day's tickets and leaflets and the activities had already begun. She reminded Iona of Ma's strict instructions and not to tarry too long before making her way to Mrs Morgan's. Then, she lifted up her skirts and ran to find Mr Barrow's stall.

* * *

Jamie's heartbeat quickened when he saw Lizzie at the door of the shed, accompanied by a large bear-like man. She was the prettiest girl he had ever seen. Her vivid red hair and high colour made her stand out from the other girls and she had a bright, energetic way of holding herself that appealed to him. He'd fancied her the moment he had pulled her soaking wet from the river water. Despite her hair plastered to her head and her clothes hung on her like rags, she was attractive. In fact, her wet clothes hadn't left much to the imagination and his body reacted as he remembered her curves and neat waist.

He was sorry she left while he explained the job to her father. He had put himself

on the line with Freddy by recommend-
ing the man for the work. Luckily Freddy
was an old romantic and felt he was
helping match-make between Jamie and
Lizzie by taking Iain MacDonald on.

'You like her, it's obvious,' Freddy had
chuckled. 'So, it's easy. Just ask her out.
Plenty of shows to go to here, eh?'

'She's pretty enough,' Jamie retorted,
trying to be casual.

Freddy snorted. 'Pretty. She's more
than pretty. If I was ten years younger — '

'Which you're not,' Jamie snapped.

'Ah, now we see the passion! You do
like her.' Freddy roared with laughter, his
eyes creased in merriment as he teased
his friend.

Jamie held up his palms with a reluc-
tant grin. 'You win. I find her attractive
but I won't pursue her.'

'What do you mean?'

'Remember what I told you, Freddy.
I have plans for after the Exhibition.
I'm saving my money and I'm going to
buy a ticket to America. They're selling
land out there cheaply. They want peo-

ple to farm it. That's where my future is. It wouldn't be fair to get involved with a girl like Lizzie when I already know I won't be around in a few months.'

Freddy shrugged, looking in the moment more foreign and less like the friend Jamie had come to rely on. Jamie set Iain to painting the hull of a gondola while he finished his own tasks. Soon, he would join Freddy and the others at the jetty. The day was brightening up and the afternoon crowd would appear, ready to be entertained. Perhaps he and Lizzie could be just friends, he mused. There was no harm in that, was there?

* * *

Iona stared at the dirty children on the river bank. They had no shoes and their clothes were ragged and filthy. Where did they live? And how had they got into the Groveries? She knew people had to pay as she had gone with Lizzie selling tickets one day earlier in the summer before Ma needed her help in the café kitchen.

She loved her mother but sometimes she wished Ma's fingers and hips didn't hurt so much. She'd rather go and play than dry dishes and run errands for Mrs Morgan when it suited her. It had been fun going around with Lizzie. She was proud to be seen with her big sister. Lizzie had a fine voice and when she called out about the shows and the events, people came and bought her tickets. Especially the young men. Iona guessed it was Lizzie's lovely long, red hair they liked. She wished she had beautiful hair like that. Hers was quite an ordinary brown. Even if Ma said it was thick and shiny and she was lucky.

The children were staring back at her. One girl, about Iona's age, stuck out her tongue. Iona gasped at her rudeness. Her dress hung off one skinny shoulder and had a tear in it so big you could see her blackened knees. A boy, who looked a bit older with hair sticking up like a brush beckoned Iona with a curl of his fingers. She turned and ran all the way to Mrs Morgan's without looking back.

* * *

Alice went straight upstairs to her room when she got home.

'I'll be with you in a moment,' she called to her aunt as she went.

Aunt Hilda had come to the front door ready to fuss over her. She was left with her mouth hanging open as Alice hurried past.

Once in her room, she came to an abrupt halt. Someone had been in. Things had been moved. Of course the maid came to tidy up and to sweep out the fireplace. But this was more than that. Her book had been opened. She picked it up. The bookmark had fallen out. She had definitely put it in last night as she had been at an exciting chapter and didn't want to lose her place. Her paintings too were slightly out of order. They were stacked against the far wall and had been in neat succession. Now, the edges of some stuck out. Alice imagined someone ruffling through them. Looking for what?

97

Her heart pounded. She ran and shut her bedroom door. She listened for a second to be certain no-one was coming. Then she dragged her chair across to the wardrobe, pulling it open. Standing on tiptoe on the chair, she was just able to reach the back of the high shelf at the top of it. She sighed with relief and brought out the piece of paper with William's first poem written in his neat draughtsman's hand. She kissed it gently. Delving into her jacket pocket she took out the new poem and laid them together. She returned them to their hiding place tucked away at the back of the wardrobe shelf.

Jumping down, she carefully put the chair back where it belonged. She didn't want to leave any clues for Maggie. For she was absolutely certain it was Maggie who had searched through her belongings. She was equally certain that her father had ordered the maid to do so. Alice knew he liked to be in control. Her stubborn refusal to marry Mr Tunbridge must have unsettled him. Probably he didn't know what he was looking for. But he was suspicious. She would have to be very careful that he didn't find out about William. Not just yet. Not until they were ready to announce they were getting married.

5

'What are you waiting for? You've been engaged to the chit for two years. Set a date and marry her. Or are you so useless you can't even manage that? You've lost one wife and you're twenty-five. Time moves on.'

Charles Tunbridge senior puffed out his curling moustaches that lay proudly on a thick nest of beard and mutton chop sideburns. The beard and moustaches were streaked with grey these days but he had an upright bearing and stocky build and excellent health for a man of fifty.

Tunbridge father and son were standing in the large drawing room at Tunbridge House. It was situated on the south side of the River Clyde but far enough away from the river traffic and the shipyards to ensure the quiet of the countryside. It meant travelling to the office every day but it was a small price to pay to escape the grime of the city and its polluted air.

'Well?' he growled, when his son didn't answer. A maid put her head round the door and scurried away when he waved impatiently at her.

'It isn't as simple as that,' Charles said. He wished he could wipe the superior expression from his father's face. Unfortunately, if he wished to keep his inheritance he had to follow the older man's demands.

'Of course it's simple,' Charles senior barked. 'Only a fool lets a woman keep him dangling. I want grandsons and I'm not getting any younger. You know the deal. It's a generous one. Once you've produced my grandson, I will transfer a number of shares in the shipyard over to you. Not only that, I will give you a large sum of money so that you and your wife can build a property to match this.'

Charles had heard all this before. His father delighted in telling him that he was a failure and useless but that he had high hopes for the next generation.

He expected to have a large say in the upbringing of his grandson to ensure he didn't turn out to be a weak-willed sissy like his son.

His father had never valued him. Charles had never heard a word of praise cross his lips. When his mother was alive, his father had scorned her too. She had been a gentle, faded woman who had brought her fortune to her marriage. She had borne her husband's ill humour with patience. As a small child, Charles had loved her. But he had grown to despise her for not standing up for herself. As he got older, he had shouted at her just as his father did.

Strangely, he had married a woman who was very similar. Elisabeth Granger had been a fragile blonde society beauty who had adored him. They had been married a year when she died in child-birth, her baby daughter dying with her. He didn't mourn her. She had irritated him after a few months, with her desire to please him.

And now there was Alice. She was

like Elisabeth in stature, being small and dainty. She was frail from her illness. Yet he sensed that she was stronger in nature than his first wife. Sometimes he felt an iron will, a stubbornness about her that flickered below the surface. He would enjoy breaking that. A wife must do what her husband wishes. She had struggled with him that day at the park. He had only wished to frighten her with the threat of a hotel and a scandal quickly hushed with a speedy marriage. He hadn't booked a hotel but the silly chit had taken flight. He was surprised when she struggled against him. Then that red-haired girl had interrupted them which angered him.

He was congratulating himself on dealing with the girl when he became aware that his father was talking again.

'She's not the only marriageable girl around. She doesn't even have a decent fortune. Henry Whittaker works for me so the girl is hardly a catch. Forget her. I'll talk to my friends at the club and we'll see if we can find someone better.'

'I want Alice,' Charles said. 'Mr Whittaker may be a manager at the shipyards but Alice's mother is an heiress and Alice will be wealthy at twenty-one when she can access her trust fund.'

Charles senior raised two bushy eyebrows. His ruddy cheeks reddened further.

'What you want is neither here nor there. Do you dare to argue with me?'

'No Father. What I meant was, I'm working on it. Alice has been ill but is much recovered. I am sure that very soon, we can be wed. Mr Whittaker is in favour of a spring wedding but he wants to discuss it with his wife. Mrs Whittaker is currently in London but will return soon.'

Charles senior puffed out his moustaches at the notion of a man discussing important decisions with his wife. Extraordinary.

'I want this sorted by the end of the Exhibition. You are one of its patrons and I understand you have certain obligations until then. But no later. If you are not married immediately after that, I will step in and find you a more suitable bride, quickly.'

'Of course, Father.' Charles masked his ill humour with a polite smile.

He needed his income and inheritance more than ever, after a few terrible evenings at his club where the cards had not gone his way. He hated fawning to his father but he promised himself that one day he would have the satisfaction of standing up to him. That day would come once he married Alice and the shares in the business had been transferred over to him, along with the money to build his house. Once Alice was with child, Charles would have all the power in his relationship with the old man. His smile was suddenly wider. All he had to do was persuade Alice to get married as soon as possible.

* * *

Alice was sketching in the drawing room when the maid announced that Mr

Tunbridge was at the door. Aunt Hilda jumped up so suddenly that the embroidery she had been sewing, flew off her lap onto the carpet.

'Tell him I'm not at home,' Alice said.

'Oh, my dear, we can't possibly do that,' Aunt Hilda said. 'He's your fiancé, after all. It wouldn't be seemly. Oh dear — '

The maid waited patiently. Aunt Hilda looked around as if to find somewhere to hide, or someone to help her. She trembled slightly and Alice felt quite sorry for her, while her own heart beat too loudly in her chest.

'Please tell Mr Tunbridge to come in,' Alice said as calmly as she could. 'And bring us tea and cake.'

She wasn't going to have the maid report back in the kitchen that Alice was afraid of her husband-to-be. Her aunt sat back with a loud thump in her chair. Alice picked up the embroidery circle and gave it to her.

'It's alright. What harm can he do here?' she said.

'Harm?' Hilda looked alarmed, 'Whatever do you mean? I don't like the man, there's something about him ... he makes me shiver but he would not do us harm.'

Alice wished she hadn't spoken out of turn. She had not told her aunt of Mr Tunbridge's attack on her at the Groveries and didn't wish to.

'No, of course not. I'm being too imaginative, but — '

'I admire your imagination,' Charles's voice interrupted what Alice had been about to say. 'Good afternoon, ladies. How lovely you both look.'

His wolfish stare seemed to devour her and Alice looked away quickly. How much had he heard? He had an uncanny ability to move silently.

'Oh, Mr Tunbridge, do come in and sit with us,' Aunt Hilda fussed, her voice quivering. 'We were just saying how much we enjoy your little visits.'

'Indeed? How kind,' Charles said, taking his seat and somehow overpowering the room with his presence.

It made Alice feel quite uncomfortable. Especially when he picked up her sketch and began to examine it closely. It was if it was her body he was roaming over. She wanted to tell him to put it down but dared not. He was the kind of man who, if he knew she disliked something, would do it more. Her father was controlling but Charles Tunbridge took it to extremes. It made her shudder inwardly at the thought of being his wife. What kind of life would that be? Driving down the panic with difficulty, she made herself speak.

'Shall I pour the tea, Aunt Hilda?'

'Yes, dear, please do.' Aunt Hilda looked incapable of that simple task. She clutched one hand within the other and her face was pale.

'I was hoping that you might take the air with me,' Charles said pleasantly. 'It is a warm, dry day and a short walk across into the Exhibition in your company would be a delight.'

Alice tried to think of a reason why she couldn't, and failed.

'What a lovely invitation,' Aunt Hilda said, taking a brave sip of her tea. 'But I'm having trouble with my legs today so can't walk too far. And Alice can't possibly go without a chaperone.'

Alice felt a wave of love for her aunt. Despite her dislike and fear of Mr Tunbridge she had tried to help.

'No need to worry, Mrs Brown,' Charles said smoothly, 'One of your maids can accompany us. I believe there's a girl called Maggie in your employ?'

Aunt Hilda frowned. 'Well, yes, there is. But how do you know her name?'

Charles chuckled as if they were all the best of friends. 'She often opens the door here or brings cigars when I visit Mr Whittaker. I find it helps bond friendships if one knows the servants.'

'Quite,' Hilda said blankly.

'That's sorted, then.' He stood up and turned to Alice. 'My dear, you will need your outdoor coat and hat. I will ask the maid to fetch Maggie. Many thanks for your hospitality, Mrs Brown. Alice will be returned to your excellent care by four o'clock.'

It was hard to believe he was the same man who had ripped at her clothes and tried to take her to a hotel. Which was the problem. Alice knew no-one would believe what had happened that day at the Exhibition if she tried to tell them. Charles knew how to behave to the outside world. He was every inch the gentleman. Only she knew how vile he was and what he was capable of. Lizzie knew too, Alice thought. Lizzie had witnessed the horror of the attack. She had a desperate urge to see the other girl again. Without Lizzie as a witness, it all felt rather unreal now.

Alice put on her coat, and slid a hat pin through her blue hat into her bun. She could hardly refuse to walk with him now. However, she would take the precaution of keeping to busy areas of the Exhibition and not letting Maggie out of her sight.

They walked down the slope from the townhouses and into the park. Charles inclined his head to the magnificent grand concert hall.

'Do you care to listen to the organ recital? Mr Herbert Walton plays each day at precisely three o'clock.'

'Another day, perhaps,' Alice said, thinking how awful to spend an hour sitting beside Mr Tunbridge, unable to escape. 'I'd like to see the Irish cottages which I haven't explored yet.'

'Very well, let us take a turn there.' He offered his arm politely and when Alice didn't immediately take it, took her hand firmly and placed it in the crook of his elbow.

She was horribly aware of touching him and tried not to show her repulsion. Behind them, Maggie followed silently. Alice thought of the search of her room. She was convinced Maggie was behind it and that Charles, not her father, had ordered it so. Especially as Charles had confessed he knew the housemaid.

The Irish cottages were part of a complete homestead. They were situated in the west of the park, next to a model farm and near to the Canadian Pavilion. They were low dwellings with thatched roofs and pretty glass bow windows. They walked round them and admired the nearby elaborate fountain. Girls dressed as Irish peasants were on show. People peered inside the bow windows to watch the cottage weavers at work. Alice was enthralled. She decided she'd come back and paint the scene.

'How are you, Alice?' Charles asked. 'Your father tells me you were ill again.'

'I am much recovered, thank you,' Alice said. Was he going to ignore the fact that he had threatened her?

'That's good. I only have your best interests at heart,' he said. 'Which is why I believe we should marry before the end of the year. Indeed, at the end of the Exhibition which is in November.'

It was as if he had never pushed her to the ground and tried to drag her to a hotel. For a wild moment she felt she had imagined the whole thing. Then she thought of Lizzie and it rooted her in reality.

'Why so soon?' she asked faintly.

'Soon?' He gave a cold laugh. 'It's

hardly that. I've waited over two years for you, Alice. Not many men would be so patient. Your father is eager for this match and so am I. You will tell your father that you want to be married this autumn and begin the arrangements.'

He placed his hand on hers with sudden pressure until her fingers tingled with pain. She tried to pull away but he was stronger. He bent his head to hers, looking to the all the world as a fond lover, as he breathed his words.

'You know what I am capable of. I will have you one way or another. You may choose. Either we have a wedding with our families present, or I take you somewhere quiet and get to know you quite slowly and thoroughly before we have to arrange a quick wedding to avoid scandal. Scandal worries me not due to my connections, but you dear Alice will suffer as your father is not quite the thing in exalted circles, is he? It's entirely your choice.'

Alice rubbed at her sore fingers and glanced around. It was so busy that no-one had heard what he said. She looked at Maggie but the maid pretended not to see her distress. Charles steered her into the Canadian Pavilion, his arm like steel around her.

'Which is it to be?' he whispered, pretending to view a display of native weaponry.

A matronly lady, dressed in a pink dress and matching cape, threw them a fond smile. Alice realised they looked like young lovers enjoying a day out at the Groveries. She wanted to weep. Maggie was smirking, showing her no respect. Alice guessed Charles was paying her for her loyalty. He had a spy in her father's house. And there was nothing she could do about it. Who would believe her?

She winced as he dug his thumb nail into the bed of her nail.

'Hurry up, I've little patience.'

'Yes, I'll marry you when you wish.' There was no choice.

'Wonderful, my darling. I will allow you and your dear aunt to decide upon a suitable date in November. Tell your father I shall call upon him soon to sort out the details. Now, I think I have had enough air for one day so we shall return you to your home.'

It was unnerving how he switched from menacing threat to polite conversation so easily. It caught her off balance and made her doubt herself. When he was being a gentleman it was as if the other side of him didn't exist. She needed Lizzie to ground her. She had to find the Highland girl again.

* * *

That morning as usual, Lizzie was up early to help Mary make breakfast. She stirred the porridge while Iona put out bowls and spoons. Mary made up hunks of dark, rough bread with dripping for Iain and Donald to take with them to work. Mrs Morgan provided lunch for Mary and Iona as part of their wages while Lizzie didn't have time to stop and eat every day so didn't take bread with her. Often she bought a pie on her way

115

round her route or didn't bother to eat at all until the evening.

The men scraped their bowls and hurried away, Donald to Harry's stall and Iain to the boat house, this morning taking Iona with him as a treat. The little girl was puffed up with importance at helping her father. Besides, she liked Freddy and Jamie who teased her and gave her sweets.

Only when they had gone, did Mary exclaim, 'Och, Donald's gone and left his piece. Will you take it to him, Lizzie darling?'

'Of course, Ma,' Lizzie said, obligingly. 'Shall I walk with you?'

Mary shook her head. 'No, I'll only keep you back. I'm that slow with the walking these days. My hip is playing up something fierce. You run ahead. I'll see you tonight.'

With a sympathetic hug for her mother, Lizzie pushed her straw boater onto her hair and dashed off. She knew where Harry's stall was but hadn't ever stopped there before. She was always too busy and had no doubt Mr Barrow's beady eyes were upon her, Harry's stall being a mite too close to Mr Barrow's own stall for comfort. But today she had an excuse to visit, if only for a fast stop.

A surly-faced girl of about Lizzie's own age was at the stall, sweeping in front of it.

'Is Donald here?' Lizzie asked. The bread was leaking in its handkerchief wrapping so she hoped he was.

'Who are you? His fancy piece?' the girl sneered.

'I'm his sister. Now is he here or not?' Lizzie snapped.

'Lizzie, what's the matter. Is it Ma?' Donald appeared from the side of the stall.

'Ma's fine, but you left your dinner.' Lizzie handed him the soggy parcel.

The girl took her brush and disappeared round the back of the stall.

'Who's that? And what's her problem?' Lizzie stood, hands on hips, ready to do battle if the girl came back. Cheeky besom.

'Och, don't mind her. That's Anna, Harry's daughter. She'd sour the milk from the cow, that one. I don't know why she's so angry.'

'Rather you than me, working with her then. I'd be hard put to button my lips if she spoke to me like that all day.'

Donald grinned. 'Aye, the fur would fly, that's for sure. Thanks for bringing my food. Lizzie — '

He called her as she turned to leave. 'Have you got a moment?'

'Surely, for you.'

'Can you look at my face. Around the eyes. What do you see?'

'I see your bonny blue eyes. What else should I see?'

'It doesn't matter.'

'Donald?'

'No, really. I'm fine. On you go, Mr Barrow is staring over here with a black scowl. I'll see you later.'

Lizzie soon forgot Donald's puzzling remarks as she took an extra large sheaf of tickets for the day. There was a special football match the following day at the new stadium and Mr Barrow told her not to return until the tickets had all sold.

She chose a route to take her to the river and the boat house so that she could pick up Iona and return her to Mrs Morgan's. Even the few pennies that Iona brought home from working in the café were useful to the family's income. All the same, Mary wanted her youngest daughter to have some freedom to enjoy the Groveries and play as a young child should. She was determined Iona was to have happy memories of her childhood, just as Mary had herself.

Iona wasn't happy right at that moment.

'Why are they so mean to me?' Iona wailed, rubbing her tear tracks from her dusty cheeks.

'Who's being mean?' Lizzie said.

'The children on the river banks. There's a girl who makes faces at me and a wee boy threw a stone.'

'Well, keep away from them, then. No-one's asking you toplay by theriver,'

Lizzie said smartly.

'I want to play by the river. Besides, there's a boy who is nice to me. He wants me to come play with them. He's the oldest and the others do as he says.'

'You're not to play with them,' Lizzie instructed sharply. 'Ma won't like it if you get too close to them or the river. Promise me.'

Iona muttered a promise but her lip curled mutinously. Lizzie pretended not to notice. She was more interested in meeting Jamie. Her father waved as she went into the boat house but carried on caulking a gondola hull.

'He's down by the jetty,' Iain called over his shoulder.

'I came to see you, Dad,' Lizzie said.

'That'll be right. I'm just dandy so off you go and find your young man.'

'He's not my young man,' she protested, but her father wasn't listening any more.

Lizzie went back out into the bright daylight. A gondola was drawing up to the jetty and Jamie was in it. She ran down to greet him with a smile.

'How are you?' Jamie smiled.

He leapt off the boat to stand beside her on the jetty and she was suddenly shy. He was so tall and broad-shouldered. Honestly, looking at him did things to her innards. It made them shiver and twist deliciously. She hoped he couldn't see the effect he had on her.

'There's a show in the Russian Village,' she gushed. She spoke too much when nervous. She knew she did. 'A troupe of Russian dancers and they say there are Cossacks and a dancing bear too. Do you fancy coming with me?'

Jamie hesitated. Lizzie's heart plummeted at his expression. He didn't like her after all. While she was busy falling in love with him, she meant nothing to him. She could have wept.

'When is it?' he said.

'Tomorrow. I've got the afternoon off.'

He seemed to deliberate with himself. Then he nodded as if he'd made a decision.

'I'll come with you. Freddy won't mind

if I take a couple of hours. I've worked more than my fair share of hours lately.'

'Meet me at the Russian Village at two o'clock?'

'See you there.'

* * *

Lizzie grabbed Iona's hand and pulled her along, humming a tune under her breath.

'What's got into you?' Iona whined, scuffing her heels and slowing them down. 'I heard you asking Jamie to the Russian show. You've never taken me yet but you promised you would.'

Lizzie stopped humming and knelt down in front of her little sister to give her a hug.

'I'm sorry, I forgot I'd promised you that. Only — I can't take you this time. It has to be just me and Jamie. I'll take you after that, I will.'

Iona brightened up. She took Lizzie's hand again and skipped alongside of her.

'I want to see the bear. I want to see

the ladies in their red costumes. They practice outside our house but it's not the same as at the show. You like him, don't you, Lizzie? That Jamie. You're sweet on him. That's alright. I like him too. He's kind and generous.'

Lizzie and Iona smiled at each other, friends once more. Lizzie left her at Mrs Morgan's Meeting Place with a happy wave. She was busy until late afternoon and, having finally sold her football tickets, headed to the Irish cottages. There were tickets for an Irish dancing event the next morning and she had to sell those as well. She reached the thatched cottages and saw people peering into the windows and admiring the recreated rural scenes. In front of the main cottage, she saw Alice, sitting at her easel, leaning forward in deep concentration with her brush.

Alice looked delighted to see her. She put down her brush and stood up.

'I looked for you earlier and couldn't find you. I decided to paint for a while and then search again.'

'Here I am. Do you want a ticket for the Irish dancing?' Lizzie asked, hopefully.

Once she'd got rid of all the tickets, Mr Barrow said she could finish up for the day.

'It's nice to see you again,' Alice said, ignoring the tickets. 'I've got so much to tell you. There's no-one else can understand the way you can. Let's take a walk.'

'What about your painting?'

Alice shrugged. 'No-one will steal it. Besides, I'm not happy with what I've painted. The perspective is all wrong. I'll have to start all over again. Please walk with me.'

Lizzie went with her. She found Alice intriguing. Her life was so very different from Lizzie's. She seemed desperate to be friends despite their difference in social status.

'You remember Mr Tunbridge?' Alice said.

Lizzie nodded. 'Has he tried anything else?'

'He has threatened to ruin me if I don't marry him in the autumn. I had to agree. If I didn't, he was going to create a scandal and marry me swiftly anyway.'

Lizzie was out of her depth. She had no experience or knowledge of how rich people went about such things. She wasn't fit to comment on Alice's quandary.

'Maybe he won't be so bad once you're married,' she said, realising Alice was waiting for her response.

'He'll be worse,' Alice moaned, 'I know it. He's cruel. Besides, I am in love with someone else. I love William. He works at Charles's shipyards. He writes me beautiful poetry. If I can't be married to William, I swear I will kill myself.'

'You mustn't become hysterical,' Lizzie said, alarmed. 'You don't mean that.'

There was a wildness to Alice's voice that she didn't care for. As if her companion was mentally frail as well as physically.

'Oh, but I do mean it, Lizzie. You're the only one who can help me.'

'Me? What can I do?'

'You're the only person apart from me

who truly knows what Charles is like. He hides his evil side to the world. He's the perfect gentleman to everyone else. He has my father eating out of his hand. My mother may dislike him but she believes him to be a good man who will provide for me. Aunt Hilda is afraid of him but doesn't know why. If I told her what he did, she wouldn't believe me.'

'I'm just a lassie, and a poor working one at that. How can I help?' Lizzie frowned.

'He has my maid spying on me,' Alice was saying, looking increasingly distracted and worried. 'I know she searched my room but she didn't find my poems.'

Lizzie didn't know what to say. Suddenly Alice clutched at her arm.

'I've got it. You can be my maid. I'll tell father that I want a personal maid. He's not going to give me Maggie as she's a housemaid. Oh, what do you say, Lizzie? Say yes, please do! It's perfect. You can help me prevent Maggie from snooping in my room and keep me safe from Charles.'

'I've never been a maid. I wouldn't know what to do or how to behave.'

'That doesn't matter. I'll teach you. It's not difficult. I'll pay you thirty pounds a year, you'll have a room in the attics, a half day off a week and three uniforms.'

But Lizzie was shaking her head. 'I can't leave my family to live with you. I'm sorry, Alice. I can't do it.'

* * *

She was still trying to forget Alice's stricken face when she got home late that evening, exhausted. Even the electric illuminations failed to please her as they usually did. Her muscles ached from walking all day and her throat was dry from calling out to sell the tickets. When she got to the little dwelling house, she didn't notice the silence as her family hunched around the rickety table. Iain was swigging from a brown bottle. There were two empties beside him. Donald looked miserable and had his arm round Iona. Mary was sitting too, the potatoes unpeeled on the table top.

'You'll never guess the job I was offered today,' Lizzie said, taking her straw boater off with relief and wiping her forehead. 'A maid's position in a posh house. Imagine that. I turned it down of course.'

Ma swivelled round. 'You did what?'

'I said no. I can't leave you all to live in a town house away from here.'

'Whoever it was, you're going to go back to them and tell them you want the position,' Mary said fiercely.

Lizzie was scared. 'What is it, Ma? What's going on?'

'Your mother's lost her job,' Iain slurred. 'Mrs Morgan has let her go.'

'But why?' Lizzie's voice was a whisper. She sat down hard on the nearest chair, the breath taken out of her.

Mary sighed. 'It's my hip and my hands and all my joints. They ache so badly I can't seem to move them well. I'm too slow to wash up and I dropped two cups today and smashed them. Mrs Morgan is a kind woman but she's a

128

business woman too and she says her business can't take it.'

Iona sniffled into Donald's shoulder. Iain looked grimly at his beer. Mary took Lizzie's hand and stroked it gently.

'So, you see, lass. There's no choice. You'll have to go into service. My prayers have been answered. We were sitting not knowing how to pay for food. Dad's pay is low and Donald's too. It's a blessing you've been offered this position. We'll miss you terribly but you have to take it. You have to.'

6

Lizzie wore her green skirt, freshly laundered, a high-necked white blouse and her straw boater hat. She didn't have much choice as she didn't own many clothes but at least she was clean and neat. Her spirits were high as she waited for Jamie at the entrance to the Russian village. She was entranced by its exotic atmosphere and the white-walled buildings with their curious tall red roofs. Around her she heard Russian being spoken. As usual, there were thick crowds of tourists thronging the area, equally intrigued by what was there to see.

'Sorry I'm late.' Jamie appeared at her side with a grin. 'Freddy found me a few tasks to complete before he'd let me away.'

Her heart flipped at the sight of him. 'Come on, then,' she said, 'the show will be starting soon.'

The theatre was packed despite it

being a hot July day. The matinee would be followed by two evening performances. Lizzie had walked past before on her way home from work, when the lights and sounds of music and laughter spilled out into the soft evening air. She knew Ma wouldn't like it if she was out late, especially with a young man. But Mary had agreed that Lizzie could go to the matinee as long as she came home immediately afterwards.

The show was as wonderful as she had hoped. There was a live band in the pit in front of the stage which played rousing Russian folk music and soon everyone in the audience was stamping their feet in time to the rhythm and clapping their hands. The dancers came on first, dressed in crimson with sprays of feathers in their headbands. They were followed by the Cossacks. Lizzie thought them very fierce with their moustaches, black hats and black and red flowing coats. They had shiny black boots which made a loud clicking on the wooden stage floor as they hunkered, arms folded and kicked out their legs in the traditional Cossack dances.

Then came the dancing bear, led by a young man in Russian dress. The band played a fiery tune that made the creature sway and growl which sent a rippling thrill through the audience. The show finished with more dancing and then a Russian choir which belted out songs in a language that no-one understood but it didn't matter as everyone tried to sing along anyway.

'That was wonderful,' Lizzie sighed as they joined the crowd flowing out of the theatre afterwards. There was a buzz of excited conversation and it seemed everybody had enjoyed themselves thoroughly.

'It was pretty good,' Jamie agreed. 'Shall we buy ice-creams at the dairy and walk over to the Machinery Hall? I haven't had a chance to see it yet but Freddy tells me they've got all sorts of trains and carriages there.'

Lizzie hesitated. She had promised Ma to go straight home. But she was having such fun and she didn't want it to end. Besides, she felt safe with Jamie. She nodded. Jamie bought them ice-creams at the working dairy farm and they walked across the covered walkway bridge to the other side of the main road and into the Machinery Hall.

They were hit with the smell of diesel and engine oil. It was a huge space with a gigantic glass ceiling. Inside were steam trains and carriages and all manner of engines on display. They passed displays by John Robertson Coach Builders and James Henderson and Company Coach Builders amongst many other stands promoting their goods. There was even a miniature railway with a blue steam engine pulling small carriages for children to have a ride on. There were squeals of delight from the children taking a tour on the purpose-built track.

In contrast, there were dark-suited gentlemen in top hats and bowler hats conducting serious business at various stands. It was obvious that while the Hall was to entertain the thousands of visitors to the Exhibition, it was also a place for the buying and selling of goods and the negotiation of contracts.

'I feel a bit out of place,' Lizzie said, licking the last of her ice-cream before it dripped onto her hand. 'I'm used to being outside in the Groveries and I haven't really visited all the attractions.'

'You haven't been to the new Art Gallery?' Jamie raised his eyebrows in surprise. 'I thought everyone had seen it by now.'

'You're making me feel terrible,' Lizzie smiled, 'I like drawing when I can get some paper but I don't like looking at paintings. I'd rather be outside enjoying the people and the sunshine.'

'Me too,' Jamie admitted. 'I like the outdoors. That's why I like working for Freddy, out on the river all day. And that's why I'm going to go to America and work my own land.'

'You're going to America?' Lizzie said, trying to hide her dismay. The day suddenly seemed duller and the sweet taste of her ice-cream melted away.

'I am, indeed,' Jamie said proudly, not noticing her reaction. 'I'm leaving at the end of the Exhibition. I'll have saved up my passage and have enough to buy a small tract of land to build a homestead and to farm.'

'Oh.' What a fool she had been. She had been dreaming of her and Jamie getting closer, maybe walking out together and all this time he had been dreaming of leaving Scotland for a better life overseas. Lizzie wanted to kick herself. Of course he wasn't interested in her. She was a skinny, red-headed poor girl with nothing to offer a man.

'What are your plans?' Jamie was saying. 'Lizzie?'

She came back to her surroundings with a start. 'What did you say?'

'Your plans for the future? You must have some.' His tone was friendly and teasing.

She wanted to slap him for not noticing her, or how she felt.

'Girls like me don't make plans,' she snapped. 'I'm from a poor family with a father who drinks and never holds a job for long. I'm about to go into service as a maid. Is that plan enough for you?'

'Sorry,' he said, looking shame-faced, 'I never thought about that. Are you really going to be a maid?'

Lizzie nodded, her anger spent as quickly as it had risen. It wasn't Jamie's fault that he had a plan for a good life that didn't include her. Life wasn't kind to girls like her. She knew that.

'I'm going to work for Alice Whittaker.'

'The girl you saved from being attacked?'

'That's right. Ma lost her job so we need the money.'

'I'm sorry about your mother. Can I help?'

Lizzie smiled. That was the Jamie she knew. Always ready to lend a hand.

'You've done enough already, getting my Dad a job and we're very grateful for that.'

'You'll be living in as a maid, won't you? Does that mean you won't be coming to the Groveries?' He frowned.

'Will you miss me?' she teased gently.

He grinned. 'You know I'll miss you. Who else will I be saving from the river?'

'Well, that's alright then,' she made her tone match his, deliberately bright and careless, 'I imagine I'll be at the Groveries most days, accompanying Alice as she paints.'

'Aye, and it'll most likely be 'Miss Alice' to you,' he said wryly. 'The upper classes like to keep people like us in our place.'

Lizzie grimaced. She wasn't looking forward to her new position despite Alice's eagerness to be friends. Jamie was right. There was a world of difference between her and the Whittakers and it would be strange new place to find herself in and adapt to.

* * *

The next morning Alice went downstairs to breakfast early, feeling energetic for the first time in a long while. She knew it was because soon Lizzie would be coming to live with her. But first, she had to get her father to agree. Because, although she had asked Lizzie to be her personal maid and the girl had agreed, she hadn't actually asked the head of the household for his permission. However, she was confident he would agree as she had a persuasive argument prepared.

Henry Whittaker and Hilda were seated at the breakfast table, one at either end. Henry was hidden behind a large sheet of newspaper, the remains of his kippers and poached eggs on the plate in front of him. The headlines were all about the ongoing war against the Boers in far away Africa.

Hilda was sipping at a cup of coffee, a half nibbled scone on her plate. She glanced up as Alice came in and patted the chair beside her.

'Good morning, dear. Come and sit with me. Cook has prepared fish and ham this morning and they are really rather good. You must eat and build up your strength. Will you take some coffee? It's still hot. Oh, I'll get the girl to bring a fresh pot. Ring for Maggie, will you dear?'

'This pot is fine, I'll help myself to breakfast this morning. Please, Aunt Hilda, don't get up. I will eat a good helping for my health.'

Satisfied that Alice was making an effort to eat, Hilda sat back with a contented sigh. At the other end of the table, Henry ruffled his papers with a cough to make it clear they were disturbing him.

'Good morning, Father,' Alice said sweetly, taking her seat with a full plate to please her aunt. 'What is the news today?'

Henry peered over the top of his newspaper with an air of disbelief. Alice rarely showed any interest in the current affairs of the country. Just like her mother. He was rather glad they did not as it saved him from conversation early in the day.

'As you are here, Father,' Alice went on swiftly, 'I wonder if I might ask you for a favour?'

Her father's brows rose slightly but he didn't rebuff her so she continued, feeling her breath caught in her chest.

'I want to employ a personal maid.'

Henry put his newspaper down and stared at his daughter. Hilda dabbed at her mouth with her napkin as his gaze swivelled to her.

'Is this your idea?' He said.

'Goodness — I — ' Her voice wavered as she searched for a suitable response. She hadn't the faintest notion whether Alice had discussed this with her before.

'It is my idea, Father,' Alice said firmly. 'I need a companion and a personal dresser. As you know, I haven't been well recently and my fatigue has returned. I need help with everyday tasks. Especially when I am soon to be married.'

She paused, having played her trump card.

Henry gave a little self-important cough. 'I'm glad to see that you have finally accepted the marriage, my dear. If your aunt deems it necessary, I can see no reason you should not have a personal maid.'

'Aunt Hilda?' Alice turned to her with

pleading eyes.

'Yes, dear. I agree it is most suitable. I will ask the housekeeper to draw up a list of girls for interview.'

'That won't be needed. I have found the maid I want.' Alice didn't go as far as to admit she had already offered the job.

Henry looked at his pocket watch. Without a further word, he left the room bound for his office at the shipyards. Employing maids was women's work and he was happy to leave the organisation to his sister-in-law.

'This is most irregular,' Hilda said in a low voice, even though no-one else was in ear shot. 'Mrs Kearns will not like it. It's her job to interview for the staff. Where did you find this girl?'

'Please, Aunt Hilda, I don't want anyone else. I like Lizzie and I feel I can trust her. She can start immediately. I'll make sure she knows her role. It will make me quite ill if I can't have her.'

'Very well, she can have a month's trial. If she is suitable, then she can stay on. Your health must come first. No man wants a sickly wife. I'll speak to Mrs Kearns and explain the situation.'

'Thank you!' Alice leapt up and hugged her aunt.

The older woman hugged her back warmly. 'Now, you have given me an unpleasant task this morning. I must face the dragon in her lair. Mrs Kearns is terrifying. Your mother deals with her much better than I ever can.'

Alice didn't care if her aunt's nerves were shredded by dealing with the staff. She had got what she wanted. Lizzie was coming to live with her. How wonderful it was.

* * *

A letter from Alice's mother arrived the same day and Henry Whittaker read it in his study that evening when John, the footman, brought it to him on a silver tray.

My Dear Henry
I am delayed in London for the fore-

seeable future. My sister, Phyllis, has broken her ankle and I am needed here to help with the household and the children. Please let Hilda and Alice know. I expect to be here for some weeks yet.

I rejoice that Alice has finally agreed to marry Charles Tunbridge this year. In your letter you raised concerns that four months was not sufficient for preparations. However, I believe that to be quite enough time, given we have waited two years for this momentous occasion. The preparations have already been made and simply need to be put into motion.

The guest list, the menus, the flowers, all this information is in a large notebook that I left with Mrs Kearns. The wedding dress is in an upstairs wardrobe, again Mrs Kearns will know where it is exactly. I will write to her myself to make certain that all is being made ready and that invitations are sent out this week.

It is unfortunate that I am down here when I should be with you all to take

*charge. However, Hilda will be able to
take the responsibility until I return.
Your loving wife
Eloise.*

Henry folded the letter and put it in
the top drawer of his desk. There was no
need to burden Eloise with Alice's previous
outbursts and attitude to marrying
Charles. Indeed, Alice had approached
him only yesterday to say she wanted to
marry him in the autumn. She had not
appeared overjoyed but Henry could
see she was being dutiful as a daughter
should be. He approved of that. Now if
Hilda was capable of carrying out her
role in organising the wedding, he could
have the peace he deserved. It was women's
business, after all.

★ ★ ★

Lizzie arrived at the Whittakers' town
house on a cool, grey morning. She
looked in awe at the immaculate stone-
work, the trimmed hedge at the front

of the property and the smartly painted black railings. Turning to the street, she had a grand view down over Kelvingrove Park and the vista of the International Exhibition laid out in the distance like a model town.

Mary had sent her off with a brisk hug and no tears. Iona had provided the tears, telling Lizzie she'd miss her. Donald patted her shoulder clumsily and her Dad had given her a sixpence with instructions not to tell Ma.

She took a deep breath and then went round to the back of the house and the servants' and tradesmen's entrance. The door was opened by a thin girl of about twelve, with straggly pale hair under a mob cap. The kitchen skivvy, she guessed.

'I'm here to see Mrs Kearns,' Lizzie said with a smile.

The girl didn't smile back. She beckoned Lizzie inside and shut the door. It clanged shut with an air of finality and Lizzie was standing in a dark hallway which smelt of beeswax and cabbage and brasses. It was cold as if the sun never found its way in there. The girl disappeared without a word and Lizzie stood unsure where to go.

A door opened on the left and a tall woman with black hair severely pinned back into a bun came out. She had dark eyes and high cheekbones and thin lips.

'MacDonald, come in here.' She gestured to the room.

Lizzie stepped inside. It was a neat sitting room with armchairs and a couch in flowered materials. There was a small fire in the fireplace despite it being summer and Lizzie was glad of it as she felt the goosebumps rise on her arms. The house was so chilly as if there was no life to it, she thought. She barely had time to notice the paintings adorning the walls before Mrs Kearns launched into a list of instructions which she did not repeat twice.

'Needless to say, I don't approve of your appointment without references. However, in this instance I have been overruled by the mistress and so I suppose we must make do with the situation.'

She sniffed to show how she felt about it.

Her mind swirling with information, Lizzie was given into the charge of the waif who had opened the door to her. Emmie took her to a large cupboard and pulled down three sets of uniform.

'You've to wear these except on your afternoon off. Then you can wear your own clothes.'

She slid a glance at Lizzie's faded green skirt. 'I'll take you up to the servants' quarters now and you can get changed. Miss Alice wants you to go to her once you're ready.'

Lizzie followed the girl up the servants' staircase, her boots clicking on the bare wood. She noticed the lack of wallpaper and how the walls had been given but a thin lick of paint. The attic rooms were stifling and airless. Emmie pushed open a door and pointed to an iron bedstead, one of two in the small room.

'That's yours. Don't go near Maggie's stuff, she'll kill you. Likes her privacy, does Maggie.'

'Where do you sleep? Are you next

door?' Lizzie clutched the bundle of uniforms to her chest.

Emmie sneered. 'You're new off the boat, ain't you. I sleep in the kitchen, stupid.'

She ran off down the stairs, leaving Lizzie in her new home. Lizzie sank down onto the thin mattress, feeling the metal springs poking up. Emmie hadn't been friendly and neither had Mrs Kearns. Maggie, whoever she was, didn't sound nice either. She felt very alone. What had she done, accepting Alice's offer?

7

'I've laid out your pink silk dress, Miss Alice, and a parasol as it's going to be a hot, sunny day.' Lizzie stood behind Alice who was seated at her dressing table, and stroked the silver-backed hairbrush through Alice's thin locks.

'I told you, you can call me Alice when we're alone,' Alice reminded her. 'Will you tie my hair up in a loose bun today please. I'm going to paint a landscape this morning of the tea rooms in front of the Horticultural Hall. There are gigantic ferns which will make a fantastic backdrop.'

Lizzie brightened. If Alice was painting, she could slip away for a half hour and visit Ma.

'I won't need you all morning,' Alice said, as if reading her mind. 'So you can visit your family.'

'Thank you. My mother isn't at all well and I'd like to see her.'

'Take her food from the kitchen. Ask Cook to make up a basket.' Alice smoothed cold cream onto her hands as Lizzie fixed her hair.

Lizzie knew that Cook was unlikely to help her. She had turned out to be just as hostile as the other staff. They resented her coming in from nowhere and getting a well paid position as lady's maid. Lizzie had overheard the cook and the housekeeper complaining about it to each other. No matter how polite and hard working she was, it made no difference to the way they treated her. Even Emmie, who was the lowest in the pecking order, made out she hated her. Lizzie didn't tell Alice this. She had quickly learned that the family and the servants, although living in the same house, lived very different lives.

Lizzie's duties were light. She had to look after Alice's clothes and do her hair. She had to keep Alice company when she was asked to. She helped serve at dinner. She was also expected to keep Alice's bedroom tidy. Maggie, the housemaid, cleaned the room and set the fire so there was no heavy work involved for her.

'Help me get dressed and then go and get ready,' Alice said. 'We'll spend the morning in the Groveries and Charles is taking me out for tea in the afternoon. After dinner, I want you to read to me.'

Lizzie sighed inwardly. Alice was greedy for her company. There were very few hours when she didn't require Lizzie with her. It was as if she was afraid to be alone. Which, in turn, meant that Lizzie was rarely alone. Sometimes she was desperate for a few minutes of peace. Those days selling tickets for Mr Barrow seemed heavenly with all the freedom that went with them.

'I don't have to tell you to be vigilant when we go to tea,' Alice said. 'I don't want to be left alone with Charles at any point.'

'I won't leave you,' Lizzie promised. She paused. 'Once you're married it'll be different, you know. He'll have you all to himself.'

Alice shuddered and went quite pale.

'I can't think of that, Lizzie. I may have agreed with Father to get married to Charles but I hope and pray it won't happen. In fact, I need you to do something for me this morning after you've visited with your mother.'

'What is it?'

Alice turned in her gilt chair so that she was facing Lizzie. Her grey eyes were huge as she spoke.

'You've been here four weeks and have settled in nicely, I think. I didn't want to burden you with too many tasks while you learnt to be my maid but now I need you to do something for me. Not just once but a regular thing. You see, I have a — a young man, William, whom I like very much. We write little notes to each other but it's so difficult to send and receive them. He works at the ship-yard offices where my father works so sometimes I can go there and see him or pass him a letter or he gives me a poem. William's a beautiful poet.'

Alice's face was almost pretty as she talked about him. There was a flush of colour along her cheekbones and her grey eyes were almost luminous. She loves him, Lizzie thought. And then immediately, how dreadful if Charles Tunbridge ever found out.

'We've got a hidey hole in a tree in the park. It's in the grounds of the Canadian Pavilion. I want you to post a note there today. I can't do it myself in case Charles is there. He's on the Executive Council of the Exhibition so he is often there.'

'Is that wise?' Lizzie asked. 'What if he finds out?'

'He mustn't,' Alice said simply. 'You can't let me down, Lizzie.'

* * *

The Groveries were a sea of ladies' parasols as the hot sun blasted the crowds. Lizzie felt the heat through the holes in her straw boater, burning her hair and scalp. She had left Alice sitting in front of her easel with a frown of concentration and a paintbrush dipped in green, ready to do justice to the fronds of palm

153

trees in front of her. She hurried home, weaving her way expertly through families and couples out to enjoy the day.

'Ma, I'm back. How are you?' she gasped as she went into the gloomy small house.

'Lizzie, darling, I'm alright but my bones do ache.' Mary struggled to rise from her chair, pulling herself up by holding onto the edge of the table. 'How is it being a maid? Does that Alice treat you right?'

Lizzie put the kettle on and made tea for them both. Mary winced as she reached for the cup but when Lizzie went to help her, she shook her head.

'I can manage just fine. It takes me a little longer, that's all. I don't want to talk about me, I want to hear about you.'

'Alice is kind and the work isn't difficult,' Lizzie said, 'but I miss my freedom. How's Dad and Donald and Iona?'

'Dad is loving working for that Freddy. He's a jolly sort and kind with it. Iona makes a bit of money at Mrs Morgan's still. As for Donald, I'm not sure what's going on with him, to be honest,' Mary said. 'He was never one for sharing his heart but he's even quieter these days. They're all busy bringing in the money for food and rent but I'm useless and doing nothing.'

'That's not true,' Lizzie cried. 'You're the one who keeps this family together. Do you need to see a doctor?'

Ma brushed this aside. 'We can't afford it and he'll only tell me what I know anyway. My joints are wearing out. I don't want you to worry about me.'

Which was like telling her not to breathe, Lizzie thought. Of course she was worried. All she could do was pour her mother more tea and sit and chat about life in the Whittakers' fancy house.

★ ★ ★

'Here, give me that,' Anna said brusquely. 'You're going to mess it up like that last one.'

Donald passed her the plate with a sense of relief. His eyesight was much worse. It had begun with a mistiness of vision on and off over the weeks. He'd tried to ignore it but now it was like he was viewing the world through a dark tunnel. He could paint most of the plates but the fine detail was difficult now. He tried to hide his problem. If Harry found out, he'd get the sack and they needed his pay more than ever with Ma sick.

'Do what you can and leave the rest to me,' Anna said when he didn't say anything. 'You can do the main landscape picture and the lettering, can't you? It's just the tiny details you can't manage.'

'How did you know?' Donald said.

Anna shrugged. 'It's obvious you've been struggling for days. You screw up your eyes when you're painting the plates, and I saw you bumping into the stall.'

'Does Harry know?'

Anna shook her head. 'He never notices stuff. Too busy making money. The stall isn't the only business he's got.'

'I can't lose this job,' Donald said. 'My mother is poorly. I need the pay.'

'We've all got our problems,' Anna said abruptly, closing off the conversation.

Donald took a deep breath and began to paint the next plate. Then he stopped and put down his brush.

'What is your problem exactly?' he said, exasperated. 'You're the grumpiest girl I've ever met.'

'If I'm grumpy it's because I have reason to be,' she said.

'Are you going to tell me about it? Because I have all day to listen. It'll take me that long to paint a perfect plate.'

She made a small sound which might have been laughter. Heartened by that, Donald faced in her direction ready to listen. He couldn't make out her expression, his eyesight was now so poor but he saw her lovely blonde hair.

'It's all Harry's fault.'

'That's another thing,' Donald interrupted. 'He's your father but you call him by his name. Why is that?'

'I call him Harry because I'm angry with him. He took me away from London when I was happy there. He's dragged me around the country to various shows and events to sell stuff. I had a boy I was in love with at home in London. We were stepping out and talking about getting married.' Anna stopped.

'He'll still be there when you go back,' Donald said. 'If he loves you, surely he'll wait for you.' He would have waited for Anna if it was him.

Anna shook her head. 'It's not him. It's me. I've been away that long, I don't have feelings for him any more. And that's Harry's fault for keeping me here. If I had never left, I'd be in love and probably married with my own home.'

'Don't you think if it was really love, you'd never stop loving him even if you hadn't seen him for a while?'

The pale disc of Anna's face turned to him. 'What do you know about it?'

'Nothing,' Donald said and picked up his paint brush once more.

The moments of understanding between them had vanished. Anna made a point of stacking the plates loudly and they didn't speak to each other again, only to the customers.

★　★　★

The Canadian Pavilion was situated near to the Russian Village. It was a stylish white building with two towers and a curved entrance roof. The Canadian flag flew proudly between the two pointed tower roofs. Beyond it to the west the university tower was visible.

Lizzie approached it nervously. She had Alice's note in her pocket. She looked over her shoulder, expecting at any moment to see Charles Tunbridge bearing down on her. She walked past a square of park railings encasing a small garden of roses and across from it and over an expanse of pebbled path, there was the tree that Alice had described. Its trunk was gnarled and thick with several cracks and a couple of small holes.

There was a family, parents and grandparents and a small boy in a sailor suit, wandering in the courtyard of the Pavilion. Lizzie pretended to admire the rose blooms until they went inside. Then she quickly went to the tree and stood on tiptoe to reach the highest hole in the bark. Her fingers scooped out a tiny, folded sheet of paper. She took Alice's note and poked it in as far as it would go. Shoving the retrieved note into her pocket, she left and walked back to find Alice.

'Here you are.' She passed her the tiny square of paper.

Alice took it eagerly. She unfolded it and read it, pressing one hand to her chest with emotion.

'It's a new poem from William. It's divine.'

She looked up at Lizzie. 'Did you leave my note? Did anyone see you?'

'I did leave it, just where you told me to. No-one saw me.'

'Good. I'll want you to do that every week. I wrote in my note that you will be our go-between. You'll make it all much easier.'

'Should you be doing this?' Lizzie said. 'Is it right to encourage William when you're engaged to another man?'

'I love William. I can't bear not to make contact with him. Maybe if Father finds out about us, it won't be terrible. Not if he sees how much we love each other.'

Lizzie thought that unlikely from what she'd seen of Alice's father.

'Dearest Lizzie, you won't let me down, will you?' Alice said, with over-bright eyes. 'I can't do this without you. You are my best friend and confidante.'

'I promise to help,' Lizzie said, soothingly.

Alice's swiftly changing moods unnerved her at times but at least she calmed when Lizzie comforted her.

★ ★ ★

In the afternoon, Charles Tunbridge came to call for Alice. She had dressed nervously, with Lizzie's help, in a dark blue skirt and cream blouse and her favourite blue hat. The hat had recently returned from the milliners where the ribbons had been replaced with new silk and the decorations now included two fine peacock feathers.

'It's lovely,' Lizzie said, as she helped Alice place the hat and carefully pin it in place.

'Thank you. I think it suits me well. Although I don't want to make myself attractive to Mr Tunbridge — Charles, as I must now call him. Should I wear my brown felt instead?'

'The brown won't match your outfit,' Lizzie said. 'Anyway, it's too late, that's the doorbell and I can hear Maggie letting him in. What do they find to talk about?'

She and Alice exchanged worried glances.

★ ★ ★

Charles's polite smile vanished when he saw Lizzie traipsing behind Alice down the stairs. Maggie had gone, called by the cook, and Aunt Hilda was in a meeting with Mrs Kearns about the following week's menus so the three of

162

them were alone.

'I thought I told you quite clearly that Maggie was to accompany you when you are out of the house.' His voice was icy.

'Maggie is busy and needed in the kitchen, and Lizzie is my personal maid. Please, Charles. Surely it makes no difference?'

Lizzie squirmed at Alice's beseeching tones. She had to stand up to him. He was a bully. Charles didn't reply but cast such a dark look at Lizzie that she shivered in spite of her thoughts.

The walk across the park from the Whittakers' house to the tea rooms was taken in silence. Charles had placed Alice's arm on his and Lizzie, walking at a polite pace behind, noticed that he did not shorten his stride for hers. Instead, Alice had to scuttle along to keep up with him. When they came to a halt outside the Palace of Industry, her chest rose and fell with her exertions. The tea room was inside on the of Palace's eight cupolas and had the most breath-taking panoramic views.

'Wait outside,' Charles ordered Lizzie.

Alice's eyes begged her not to leave but Lizzie had no choice. She could hardly keep them company. She sat on a low wall outside the grand building and angled her face to the sun. She thought of the look Mr Tunbridge had given her. Well, if he hoped to bully her, he'd failed. She was furious instead and resolved to protect Alice from his nastiness. At least he couldn't do much to Alice in a tea room.

She waited for an hour before they emerged. Charles ignored her while Alice gave her a small smile. She followed at a respectful distance as he escorted Alice back to the house. When Alice went upstairs to rest, he caught Lizzie's arm.

'I know who you are,' he said, as she tried to pull away. 'You're the girl who interfered the day Alice and I were arguing.'

'Arguing. Is that what you call it?' Lizzie managed to get her arm free and stood back from him, the staircase banister hard against her back. 'You attacked her. What kind of monster does that?'

'You're just an ignorant peasant from the hills. You misunderstood what you were seeing.'

'I know what I saw,' Lizzie said, refusing to be afraid even though her heart beat painfully in her chest.

He leaned forward until his face was right at hers. She shrank back but could go no further. His breath was hot on her face and the pores of his skin visible.

'You don't want to cross me, girl. I'm warning you. I won't give a second warning.'

A door slammed somewhere in the house and he turned away from her toward the front door. The door shut behind him and Lizzie took a deep shuddering breath. She composed herself and started up the stairs. Through the banisters she saw John, the footman, in the hall. How long had he been there? Had he witnessed Charles's threatening gesture? He was facing straight ahead as he was trained to do, but as Lizzie went up to find Alice, he tilted his head and watched her go.

Lizzie was bored and glad when Alice finished reading that evening. She had to read out loud. Alice didn't mind that Lizzie stumbled over words and was slow at reading. She was happy to prompt and correct her. Now, Alice slumbered in her chair. She woke with a little jerk.

'I'm going to bed. I don't need you further tonight, dear Lizzie.'

Lizzie went to her own bed up in the attic. There was no sign of Maggie, which was a relief. She was restless. Outside the attic window, she saw it was still day light as it was the peak of high summer. On an impulse she grabbed her shawl and slipped out of her room. She wasn't meant to leave the house unless it was her afternoon off but she wanted to see Jamie. All she had to do was let herself out of the back door without being noticed. She'd be seen but if she went casually, perhaps they might think she was on an errand for Alice.

As it turned out, no-one saw her. The other servants were in the servants' dining room, talking and drinking hot chocolate. Lizzie smelt the sweet scent of it as she slipped past. Not that she was ever offered any by Cook. She went out by the back door and pushed it closed, quietly. She prayed that it wouldn't be bolted when she came back.

She joined the evening revellers coming out of shows and concerts. The Grand Illuminations were lit despite the daylight and glittered prettily across the buildings. They were more dramatic in the darkness as they had been earlier in the year but she liked them anyway. Her feet took her along the river path to the jetty before she stopped. She had no idea where Jamie lived. If he wasn't at the boat house, she had no idea where to search for him. Luckily, there were two figures at the boat house as she ran the last stretch of the path. Freddy and Jamie were closing up for the evening as she arrived.

'Ah, bella Lizzie. How are you?' Freddy called.

'What are you doing here so late?' Jamie grinned.

Both men looked tired, their shirt sleeves rolled up on muscled arms and a glistening of sweat on their brows.

'I thought you might like a walk before the Groveries shut for the night,' she said.

Freddy chuckled and pushed Jamie playfully towards her.

'My friend, you listen to Lizzie. I can finish up here by myself. Enjoy the beautiful evening together.'

'Thanks, Freddy. I'll come early tomorrow to make up for it,' Jamie said.

Lizzie took his hand and pulled him along with her on the path, waving back to Freddy cheerfully.

'Does Alice know you're here?' Jamie asked.

'No, but what she doesn't know, can't hurt her,' Lizzie said airily.

Then, more seriously, 'I had to get out of there, Jamie. That house — the atmosphere claws at my throat. The servants hate me, I'm sure Maggie goes through my belongings, and Alice is — Alice is never far from me, like she's my shadow or I'm hers.'

'I'm sorry it's awful,' Jamie said, squeezing her hand sympathetically. 'Work isn't ever fun.'

'That's not what you told me about working for yourself,' Lizzie said with a smile.

'That's true. It's different then. You work hard and you're rewarded for your labours,' he said. 'I've moved things on a bit.'

'What do you mean?' Lizzie asked, hearing the excitement in his voice.

'I've booked my passage on the SS Astoria, leaving on the fourteenth of November.'

'Going to America?'

'Going to New York. From there, I'll have to travel overland.'

'Oh, Jamie. I'll miss you.'

'I'll miss you too.' His face fell. 'Only, this is my dream, Lizzie. I can't give it up. Not even for you.'

'And I wouldn't ask you to,' she said. 'It's not as if we're stepping out together or made a promise to each other, like marriage.'

'No,' he agreed, slowly.

He stopped on the river path. There was no-one about as the crowds thinned. The Exhibition shut at 10pm and it was nearly that hour. The river water lapped on the shingle edges and a duck flew past with a squawk. Jamie put his palms on either side of her face, leaned in and kissed her. Lizzie's mouth opened in surprise and he took that as an invitation to deepen the kiss. She pressed her fingers to the warm nape of his neck and pulled him closer. His body responded and she felt an urge, strong and primitive rise up in her for more. More of what, she wasn't certain. She only knew she loved the feel and taste of this man and never wanted to let him go.

Jamie drew back for a ragged breath. Lizzie touched her mouth, wonderingly.

'Sorry, I had no right to do that,' he said.

'Did you see me trying to stop you? I liked it too.'

'But, we've just agreed there is no promise between us. I shouldn't have

170

taken advantage of you.'

Lizzie made a rude noise in her throat. 'Don't be daft. You haven't taken advantage. It takes two to kiss, doesn't it? In fact, I'd like to try it again. There's no promise, we're both agreed but there is the rest of the summer and autumn before you leave. Let's not waste it.'

'Are you sure?'

For an answer, she drew him close once more and practised her kisses again.

* * *

Her mouth felt tender and tingling as she let herself back into the town house and she was happy as she had never been before. The back door was thankfully unbolted and she crept in to the dark corridor. Everyone had retired to bed. She tiptoed past the sleeping form of Emmie, lying in front of the range in the kitchen and made it as far as the ground floor. Someone loomed out of the darkness with a flickering candle before she made for the stairs.

'Lizzie, is that you?'

'Alice! You gave me a heart attack. What are you doing, wandering around down here?'

'I could ask you the same question. I've more right to do so than you,' Alice said. 'Where have you been?'

'Let's go upstairs,' Lizzie whispered. 'Someone might hear us.'

Alice padded up the stairs with Lizzie following.

She turned in to the parlour and sat in one of the armchairs, pointing at the other. Lizzie sank into it.

'Where have you been?' Alice asked again.

'I'm sorry, I know I'm not meant to leave the house but I needed fresh air. I went for a walk in the Groveries.' Lizzie didn't say she had met Jamie. She wanted to savour the memory of his kiss all to herself.

'I couldn't sleep,' Alice said. 'I got up and walked around the house. I do it quite a lot in the night. No-one's around and it's so peaceful somehow. But I'm

172

tired now.'

'Do you want me to help you to your bed?'

Alice shook her head. 'I'm used to it. I haven't slept well since my illness two years ago.'

'What were you ill with?' Lizzie asked.

Alice had never gone into details of her illness and her aunt, when instructing Lizzie on her duties, had nervously avoided any mention of why Alice was delicate and required meticulous care.

'You don't have to tell me,' Lizzie said, 'I shouldn't have asked.'

'It started with a fever. Just around the month after I had accepted Charles's proposal. He had seen me with my father at the shipyard office that spring and fell in love with me immediately. I was flattered. He was older than me and very sophisticated. I was fresh from my coming out where I had met no-one who interested me. He was always there, taking me out to dinner and shows and for promenades. After a matter of a few weeks, he asked my father for my hand in marriage. He began to unnerve me in some way. I can't describe it exactly. Whatever it was I sensed, I drew away. He hated that and was sharp in his tone. You know what he's like, Lizzie. You've seen what he's capable of. He began to show his true nature. I wanted to end the engagement and he went into a rage. He threatened me with all sorts of dire things if I should break it off. Then I got sick.'

'How awful,' Lizzie murmured, shifting closer to Alice and taking her trembling hand.

'After the pneumonia was over and the doctor said I was out of the woods, I was so very tired. I lay in bed all day and could not rise. Charles tried to bully me out of it whenever my mother allowed him to visit. She stopped the visits when she saw they made me worse. But I was so unhappy. I gave up.'

'What do you mean you gave up?'

'I stopped eating and washing and went into what you would call a decline. I think I didn't want to live any more.

It was very frightening for Mother and Father.'

'But you got better?' Lizzie prompted, when Alice stared ahead of her silently. She stroked the other girl's cold hand, trying to warm it.

'In the end, I did get better. In spite of myself. This spring, the sunshine and warmth brightened me and my strength is returning. Of course I have my little cures which help. I don't have so many dark thoughts now. Meeting William has changed me. I'm in love with him. He makes me happy in a way that Charles never can.'

Lizzie couldn't bring herself to ask what would happen when Alice married Charles and William was out of reach forever. Alice believed a miracle was going to happen to deliver her from her fiancé into her lover's arms. Lizzie knew the world worked differently. Her family had struggled for every small thing they had. Happiness could be fleeting.

8

Alice woke feeling sluggish. She had taken a small dose of laudanum to help her sleep after saying good night to Lizzie. She sat up in bed and reached for her shawl to wrap around her shoulders. When she rang the bell, Lizzie quickly appeared.

'Pass me the Fowler's Solution please,' Alice said.

Lizzie picked a small brown bottle from the medicines on the bedside table and gave it to her.

'That's better,' Alice sighed. 'It tastes quite bitter but does me the power of good. I can feel my energy returning. And I shall need it today. I'm meeting William this afternoon down by the river.'

'Is that wise? Isn't there a risk that Charles will see you?' Lizzie laid out a towel beside the jug of hot water for Alice to wash with.

'We should be safe. Charles told me yesterday that he has meetings all day today at the shipyards. William has a half day so he won't be expected in work. It's perfect.' Alice clapped her hands at her own cleverness.

'All those notes you had me fetch from the tree this week, was that the planning of your tryst?'

'Yes, indeed. I couldn't manage that without you.' Alice washed her face and hands, enjoying the heat of the water on her skin.

'Will you be wanting me to accompany you this afternoon?'

'Yes. Once William arrives you must stay nearby and keep a look out in case Charles has changed his plans.' Alice shivered and stretched out her arms. 'Look, I have gooseflesh. It's cold in this room. Call Maggie and have her make up the fire.'

'Your aunt disapproves of fires in the bedrooms in summer,' Lizzie said.

'It's hardly summer now that it's September. I'm frozen. Call for Maggie. You can help me dress and I'll have a small breakfast to please Aunt Hilda although I have no appetite. That will give Maggie time to search my room and report to her master.'

'You're convinced she does sneak about?'

'You aren't?' Alice asked. 'I know someone periodically moves things around in here. I can tell, even when they place everything back. I lay out my book, my medicine bottles in a certain way and when I return they are differently placed. Who else can it be? I know that Maggie tells Charles about me.'

'I believe you,' Lizzie said. 'She hasn't warmed to me at all since I came here. She seems to view me as the enemy.'

'You are the enemy,' Alice laughed. 'Because you're on my side.'

She looked at Lizzie properly and saw a sadness there. She patted the bed. 'What is it, Lizzie? Come and sit beside me and tell me. We're friends, aren't we? Friends tell each other what's on their mind.'

'It's nothing,' Lizzie said, but coming to sit beside Alice as commanded.

'Come along, there's something,' Alice coaxed.

She loved Lizzie but also had a selfish reason for wanting her to be happy. If Lizzie was happy she wouldn't want to leave her. Sometimes, she thought if it wasn't for Lizzie's friendship she'd fall apart entirely and no Fowler's Solution nor swig of laudanum could save her.

'I cannot fit in to this household,' Lizzie said. 'I've tried to be friendly, I carry out my tasks but I can please no-one.'

'You please me. That must count for something.'

'But I have to live with the others. It can be — difficult.'

'I'll ask Aunt Hilda to have a word with Mrs Kearns.'

'No! No, please promise you won't. That might make it worse if they think I've told you. I'm no tell-tale.'

'Very well, though I think it a mistake.

179

Servants must do as they're bid,' Alice said.

'I'm a servant too.'

'I didn't mean you,' Alice cried, hugging Lizzie, 'I don't think of you like that. Come along now, let's cheer up by deciding what I'm going to wear today. I want William to find me attractive.'

Lizzie selected day wear and spread it on the bed for Alice to choose.

'What do you suggest?' Alice said, hoping to brighten Lizzie's strange mood and distract her. 'The green silk is pretty. Or the black and white striped skirt?'

In the end, she chose the green silk day dress with its high-buttoned neck and delicate cuffs. There was a matching cape which was welcome as the day was cooler than usual.

'Perhaps I shall join you this afternoon,' Aunt Hilda said at breakfast, cutting a scone in half and spreading it liberally with butter. 'The weather is fine and I haven't been to the Exhibition for a while. I'm not making the most of my season ticket.'

Alice paused in the middle of crumbling a scone to pieces on her plate, disguising her poor appetite. How was she to meet William with her aunt fussing around her? Aunt Hilda was vague in manner but had a sharp set of eyes nonetheless. She remembered people's faces and fashions in minute detail when gossiping with her friends.

'I heard it is to rain this afternoon,' Alice lied.

'How disappointing. I don't think I will go. You shouldn't either. You might get a chill or worse.'

'If it rains, I'll take shelter in the Palace of Industry where it's warm and dry.' Alice knew her aunt disliked the Palace.

As if on cue, Aunt Hilda gave a dramatic shudder. 'I hate that place. The statue there does our king no favours. It gives one the feel that he is a hunchback. As for the ferns, they make me sneeze. No, I will not go with you. I'm sorry, Alice dear, I've let you down, I'm afraid.'

'You mustn't worry, Lizzie will be with me. I shall be fine.'

'The girl has worked out well after all,' Aunt Hilda said, finishing her scone and reaching for another. 'She's a little rough round the edges but does her tasks and never answers back.'

'She is more of a companion than a maid,' Alice said.

Aunt Hilda looked alarmed. 'Oh, no, my dear. She's hardly that. A companion is refined and able to discuss on a number of educated subjects fit for a young lady. Even to discuss the latest news from home and abroad. A companion comes from a good family. If you are looking for one, my dear friend, Miss Christopher, has a cousin who has fallen on hard times and is looking for such a position. I can enquire — '

'Please don't ask her,' Alice said, 'I'm perfectly happy with Lizzie's company. She can read, if bumpily, and I enjoy correcting her and teaching her new words.'

Aunt Hilda raised her eyebrows but said no more on the subject. At least talking about companions meant she hadn't noticed that Alice had eaten nothing.

She had managed a cup of weak coffee and cream. The morning went by slowly. She embroidered, played the piano and read her novel but all she could think about was William.

* * *

Alice was relieved to find the footpath by the river busy with people that afternoon. She walked slowly along beside the water. The weeping willows' leaves rippled in the breeze and ducks bobbed on the river surface. She lifted her face to the sun for a moment.

'Isn't this lovely?' she said to Lizzie. 'You can leave me here. William knows where to find me. But don't go far away. Keep your eyes open for trouble.'

She watched Lizzie walk away. Her heart pounded. Where was he? Then she saw his tall figure coming towards her. He was smiling. He reached her and stood awkwardly, a small posy of flowers in his hand. He offered them to her.

'These are for you.'

'They're beautiful, thank you, William.' It was a thrill to say his name, to let it roll deliciously from her lips.

'Shall we walk?' he said and she realised he was as nervous as her.

'Are you afraid we will be seen?' Alice breathed in the scent from the flowers and glanced at him.

'I could lose my position if Mr Tunbridge finds out that we've met,' William said.

'But you came anyway.'

'How could I not? You – you are so lovely, Alice. I cannot resist. Even if it's wrong.' He shook his head as if impatient. 'I am gone completely mad.'

'You're not mad,' Alice said, putting her hand on his arm in comfort, then taking it away. They must not touch. If Aunt Hilda changed her mind and came to the Groveries, Alice might explain her chatting with William away as a chance meeting but not if they were showing affection to each other. 'Or, if you are, then I am mad too. I had to see you again.'

He began to walk along the path and she went beside him. They walked slowly so that they could chat easily. There were many other couples doing the same so they blended in nicely.

'Are you well?' he asked politely.

'I am much better for seeing you,' she said. 'Let us not wast time on niceties. Tell me about yourself. Have you brothers or sisters? Do you have parents yet? What is your favourite dessert? There is so much to find out.'

'I am the youngest of three sons and yes, my parents are alive. My oldest brother is a doctor, the middle one a lawyer and I was destined for the church. I had to persuade my parents to allow me to study as a draughtsman. I love ships. As for dessert, almond cake is my favourite. Now it's your turn,' he smiled.

'I am an only child. I had two younger sisters but they died as babies. I think that's why my Mama is always concerned about my health. She is in London just now, looking after her sister, but she writes often and asks how I am. She doesn't ask what I do, but whether I am well, how long do I sleep, am I eating and so on.'

'It must be terrible to lose a child.'

'Yes, but I wonder if her obsession with my health makes me obsessive too. I am, I suppose, a semi-invalid. I go to bed early and there are days when I do not get up at all. I'm not a good catch as a wife.' Alice looked to see his reaction. Their hands brushed briefly as they moved out of the way of another couple on the path and she felt a tingle rush all the way up her arm.

'Do not say that,' William said. 'You are creative and imaginative and clever. I would never tire of you if you were my darling wife.'

Alice quivered under his searching gaze. 'Dare we dream and hope of it?'

His warm hazel eyes darkened miserably. 'We dare not. You are to be married this autumn. We should not be conversing nor swapping notes and poems. It's disgraceful by all standards. I should feel ashamed but strangely I do not.'

'Neither do I,' Alice cried. 'Dear William, I am ashamed only that I am engaged to Mr Tunbridge. Oh, if there was only a way out. There must be! Can we not think of something? Make a plan in some way?' She balled her hands into fists, full of raging emotions usually too strong for her body and mind. William made her strong. He made her feel full of life.

'I wish it were possible,' he groaned. 'Are we making this worse than it has to be? More sensible that we should not meet or communicate at all. But this I can't bear.'

'Nor me. I cannot give up hope, even if there appears to be none.' She thought for a moment. 'What if I were to break off my engagement?'

'No, you can't do that. It would cause a scandal and your reputation would not recover.'

'We could elope,' Alice said.

'Our families would cut us off. I am not wealthy and do not earn enough to keep you as you are used to. It's no good.

We must accept our fate. This is the only time we have together. A few months at most.'

Alice said no more on the matter and they walked along, enjoying each other's company and chatting about poetry and art. She thought that Aunt Hilda might sympathise and resolved to discuss the matter with her. If her aunt reacted well, she might talk to Alice's father and persuade him that her happiness was more important than his connections to wealth and titles. She didn't waste a moment considering Charles's feelings as she was convinced he had none. No decent feelings at any rate.

* * *

Charles at that very minute was tucked away in a leafy lane behind the Whittakers' town house speaking to Maggie. His business at the shipyards concluded, he had arranged to see her.

'You searched thoroughly?' he was asking her.

'Yes, Sir. As you ordered, I go through her room each day looking for anything out of the ordinary. I'm that careful putting stuff back she never notices.'

'Not a letter or a postcard? No new pieces of jewellery or perfume?' Charles said impatiently.

Maggie shook her head. 'Nothing, Sir.'

He was frustrated. If only he could search Alice's room himself instead of relying on a foolish maid to do so. He sensed Alice had a secret. She was holding something back from him. There was no proof but his sixth sense told him so. It had never let him down in the past. Why else was she resisting him? She felt she had an alternative. That was his guess. The question was, what was that alternative? And, how much of a threat to him was it? Alice belonged to him. She had to learn that lesson, fast.

'I want you to keep looking. When you find something, I want to know immediately. Is that clear?'

Maggie bobbed a curtsey. 'Yes, Sir. Of course.'

'I don't need to remind you to tell no-one of our little arrangement. If I should find you've opened your mouth …'

Maggie looked frightened and he smiled without humour. He turned on his heel to leave.

'Please, Mr Tunbridge, Sir. You haven't paid me,' Maggie called.

He turned back with a sneer. 'Why pay you when you haven't achieved anything?'

'There is something —'

'What? Spit it out like a good girl.'

'She went to the Groveries this afternoon. I heard her putting off Mrs Brown from going with her. She was happier than usual as if she had something to look forward to. She was going to the river.'

Charles felt in his pocket for coins and threw them at her. He watched as Maggie scrabbled on the ground for them.

'Good. I'll be visiting here again soon. Make sure you have a decent report for me.'

With his long stride, Charles was soon at the river. The gondolas floated past him both ways, their occupants laughing and waving. He ignored them. Where was she? He stood at a bend in the river, looking in both directions. It wasn't easy to find a particular person as people streamed past. Luckily he was a head taller than most. He walked up the slope for a better vantage point.

There she was. He saw her blue hat, its feathers swaying in the breeze. She was wearing an emerald dress and carrying a folded parasol. As he fixed his attention on her, he realised she was talking to a sandy-haired man beside her. Even as he watched, she put out her hand and touched the man's arm.

An icy rage surged through him. The boldness of her, flaunting herself in public with another man, when she belonged to him. He had to know the interloper's identity.

At once, he set off down the slope,

keeping his gaze fixed on her. People got in his way and he pushed through them, ignoring their protests. One man began to argue but when he saw Charles's expression, he melted away into the crowd.

He was almost upon them when a band of Scottish pipers, clad in garish tartan and belting out a Highland lament, marched through the crowds. Suddenly he lost them on the other side of the marching pipers. He wasted precious minutes waiting for a break in the procession to get through. The crowds applauded and called for more tunes. The pipers passed by with children running after them, and he was free to move across to where Alice had been. He cursed. He was too late. The sandy-haired man had vanished. Alice was nowhere to be seen either.

He hesitated. He could go after Alice and let her know what he'd seen. Beat it out of her if necessary. There was a flash of red hair ahead. Alice's maid. He decided not to challenge Alice. Better to wait, knowing what he now knew. He had been right. She had a secret. Except that now he knew her secret too. And, he'd find a way to identify her lover. For what else could the man be? He'd bide his time before pouncing. Alice was going to marry him and no-one was getting in the way of that.

* * *

'I swear it was Charles,' Alice fretted, later that evening.

'Stop, you'll wear a track in the carpet if you keep pacing like that,' Lizzie said.

They were in Alice's bedroom. Alice was in her night dress and Lizzie had been combing her hair until Alice leapt up in agitation.

Lizzie sighed and put down the silver-backed brush. 'Go through it again so I can imagine it.'

'I told you. I was saying goodbye to William and I felt a prickle on the back of my neck as if I was being watched. I looked around and I'm sure I saw Charles. Just for a second before the military band went past. When the band had gone, so had he.'

'It can't have been him,' Lizzie said. 'You told me he was at meetings in the shipyards all day. It must have been a man who looked like him. All these toffs wear the same dark suits and bowler hats.'

'I hope you're right,' Alice muttered.

'Come and sit at the dressing table so I can brush out your hair. I only reached thirty strokes before you jumped up.'

'What if it was him?' Alice trembled. 'What if he saw William? He's capable of terrible actions, I know he is.'

'What if the moon is made of green cheese?' Lizzie teased gently. 'Dear Alice, you're worrying too much about nothing. If it was Charles, don't you think he'd have come and accosted you? He'd have been furious and if there's a man who cannot control his temper, I'd say it's your Mr Tunbridge.'

Alice's shoulders went down. 'You're right. It can't have been him, can it? Tell me it's so, Lizzie.'

'It is so,' Lizzie soothed, brushing Alice's fine, fly-away hair until it crackled with electricity. 'You're worrying for nothing and it isn't good for your health.'

Lizzie was fairly certain that Alice had imagined the whole episode. She was prone to anxiety. If Alice was to sleep at all that night, she had to put the idea out of her head. And so did Lizzie.

'Thank you. Here, take some paper for your sketching and a couple of my pencils,' Alice said. 'Good night.'

Lizzie hugged the spontaneous gift in delight. She rarely had paper and her only pencil was but a stub. She left Alice tucked up in bed and decided to go down to the kitchen for a glass of water before heading up to her attic bedroom.

* * *

Below stairs was quiet. Lizzie passed the servants' dining room and heard chatter. She saw Mrs Kearns in her sitting room. She promptly shut the door as Lizzie went by. There was no-one in the kitchen. Cook had finished up for the day. There were piles of vegetables, freshly prepared for the next day and pies made up ready for the ovens. Lizzie's tummy rumbled. She was always hungry.

Never mind. Sketching took her thoughts away from food. She drew from memory images of the Groveries, with Jamie and his gondola, the trees and the musical bands. She drew the bowl of vegetables. She was so engrossed, she didn't notice Emmie come in to the kitchen until she felt her hot breath on her ear and smelt her faintly sour body odour.

'Them's just like real life,' Emmie said, 'the carrots and onions and whatnot. It's like magic.'

Lizzie laughed. 'It's not magic. Anyone can draw, given half a chance. Here, take this pencil and wee piece of paper and give it a go.'

'I can't.' Emmie sounded appalled.

'Yes, you can. Go on,' Lizzie said, pushing the pencil into the girl's fingers. 'Draw what you like.'

'I can't write.'

'That's alright, because I'm not asking you to. Drawing's different from writing.' Lizzie pretended to focus on her own drawing but watched out of the corner of her eye as Emmie hesitantly put the tip of the pencil to the paper.

The minutes passed in silence except for a dripping tap and the distant sound of laughter from the dining room. It was a joy to draw, to let her mind escape this house and its occupants for a little while. Beside her, Emmie's breath was laboured and a whiff of armpits wafted over. The girl's tongue hung out in concentration.

'There.' Emmie slid her paper across to Lizzie.

There were two stick figures at a rectangle and some squiggles in the corner of the paper. Emmie pointed. 'It's you and me at the table drawing. Them's the pies on the side waiting to be cooked.' She sounded proud and slightly embarrassed.

'I like it,' Lizzie said. 'It's telling a story

as a good picture ought to. Well done.'

'It's not as good as yours,' Emmie said, enviously.

'No, it's not. But that's because it's your first attempt. You'll get better, just as I did.'

Emmie stared at her for a long moment. Then she said, 'Want some hot chocolate? Cook made up a jug. I can heat it up.'

Lizzie's eyes welled up. She rubbed her nose and sniffed. 'I'd like that very much. Thank you, Emmie.'

'You're not so bad. Maggie says you're a dirty peasant but she's wrong. I like you. I'm sorry I've been mean.'

Emmie was only the kitchen skivvy and the lowest in the servants' ranking but Lizzie felt finally accepted. She had made her first friend here. Surely, in time, she'd win the rest of them over.

9

'It's that good to see you, come away in,' Mary said with a smile.

Lizzie saw how it pained her Ma to walk from the door to their room. It was only a short distance but she laboured over it.

'Don't worry about me,' Mary said, glancing at Lizzie, 'I'm just fine. A few aches, that's all.'

'You don't need to soften it for me, Ma,' Lizzie said. 'I can see you're suffering. I wish I could do something. Shall I fetch the doctor to you?'

Mary shook her head. 'A waste of money. No doctor can cure me. I've to learn to live with it, and I will. Now, let's talk of more interesting things. What's it like living at the big house?'

Lizzie filled the kettle and put it on the old range to heat. No matter what Ma said, she was worried about her. Her mother was so brave. She never complained. Lizzie hoped she'd be as courageous if it was her.

The room was looking more homely than when she last visited. There was a new rag rug on the floor and two new pottery cups. Mary saw her looking.

'With your Dad's pay and yours, I've managed to get a few items. Pour the tea in those pottery cups. I got them from a stall for cheap as they're chipped. You can't see the damage so I got a bargain.'

She took her cup of tea and sat carefully, looking at her daughter. 'Are you happy with that Alice? Is she good to you?'

Lizzie sipped her hot tea, burning her lip. She set it down before answering.

'Alice is friendly. She likes me and I like her but she's fragile as if a puff of wind would blow her away.'

'She's gentry so don't go getting too friendly. They stick together when it goes wrong,' Mary said, clasping her cup and feeling the heat soothe her bones.

'I don't think Alice is like that,' Lizzie said, 'I've more problems with the other servants to be honest.'

'Why's that? You're a good girl, always truthful, kind and helpful.'

'There's one maid, Maggie, who's stirring trouble for me. I don't know why but she's turned them against me. I've made one friend there but she's just the kitchen skivvy with no influence on the rest of them.'

'Do you remember Fiona MacDougall from Inverbuie?'

'I think so. She was your friend, wasn't she? Older than you by a few years. What about her?'

'Happen she came to Glasgow to be a cook for a grand family up near the Whittakers' part of town. I'll have a word with her. The cooks all know each other from what I hear.'

'Thanks, Ma. I didn't know you kept in touch with her.'

'We write a few letters a year to each other. We're not best friends but she's a nice woman. She'll be able to talk to the cook in that Alice's house.'

'How are Dad and Donald and Iona?'

Lizzie asked, taking the conversation away from herself. She didn't want Ma to worry about her. Also, she hadn't seen her family in a while. It was hard to get away from Alice's needs even on her half day a week, and on her day off on Sunday she often went walking with Jamie.

'Your Dad is fine. He loves working with Freddy at the boat house. He has a few drinks still but not so much he gets maudlin. Iona is growing up fast. She's working at Mrs Morgan's coffee house doing my job so gets more pay. When she's free, she's down at the river. Says she likes the freedom there.'

'She should be here after work, helping you,' Lizzie said, sharply. 'I'll have a word with her.'

'Och, leave her be.' Mary shook her head. 'She's young, she needs some fun and she'll hardly get that in the house with me of a day. I can manage. Besides, she's home early evening to make the dinner.'

'What about Donald? How's he doing? I've hardly seen him in weeks.'

'That one, I do worry about. He's that quiet, I'm sure something is bothering him but he says not. He should be happy, he's seeing a girl called Anna, but it doesn't seem to cheer him up none.'

'He's seeing Anna? That's Harry's daughter at the stall. I didn't know that. Maybe the path of true love isn't running as smooth as it might.' Lizzie grinned. 'Donald's always been a quiet lad. He's probably fine, Ma.'

Mary smiled. 'I met her when she walked him home. She's done that lately, it's become regular.'

'He will be. Mind you, that Anna is a right sour puss. What he sees in her, I can't imagine.'

'Lizzie MacDonald, you're terrible.'

But Mary was laughing and it cheered Lizzie up to see her doing so. She left the little house feeling brighter and more positive. Alice's fears about Charles cast a dark shadow every day that pervaded their hours together. Lizzie hadn't realised how affected she was by it until she left the Whittakers' and came to see her mother. She felt the outline of folded paper in her pocket. She had to leave a message for William in the usual tree on her way back to the house. She wasn't meant to be visiting Mary, she was supposed to be picking up messages – another bottle of Fowler's Solution from Alice's doctor and a pair of gloves that Alice had ordered from the milliner's on the main road.

Humming a little tune, she shifted the basket on her arm and set off, unaware of the figure behind her, following her steps.

★ ★ ★

Alice waited until her father was out of the house before talking to Aunt Hilda. She had spent days building up her nerve to discuss William with her. Surely, Aunt Hilda would understand? She disliked Charles almost as much as Alice did. She'd want her niece to marry someone she loved.

Aunt Hilda was taking afternoon tea

with her good friend, Miss Christopher. Tall, thin Miss Christopher with her long, pointed nose and extravagant headwear had brought her small dog with her. A faint smell of damp dog hair hung in the air outside the parlour. Alice knew the two ladies were discussing Miss Christopher's summer wedding plans for the following year. As she stood there, the door opened and they came out.

'There you are, Alice,' Aunt Hilda said, her cheeks flushed from a glass of afternoon sherry. 'You should have joined us. Mavis was describing her wedding dress in great detail to me.'

'I wasn't feeling well so I lay abed late,' Alice said.

'Goodness, will you be well enough for your own wedding?' Miss Christopher peered at her. 'I believe congratulations are in order. Such a short while to prepare for your wedding day, although your aunt assures me all is in hand.'

The small dog sniffed at Alice's hem. She pushed it gently away with her foot, hoping its owner wouldn't notice.

'I'm sure I'll be quite well, thank you. I'm sorry I missed hearing about your dress.'

The smell of the dog was making Alice feel sick. She was glad she hadn't had to sit through wedding dress descriptions and pretending to feel excited about her own wedding or that she was in love with Charles.

'Thank you for the tea,' Miss Christopher said to Hilda. 'Let us meet again next week.'

Hilda saw her friend out of the house and turned back to Alice.

'It is a love match. Very romantic. Miss Christopher was firmly on the shelf at thirty, a confirmed spinster when the Reverend Moles arrived in her neighbourhood. He took one look at her and declared himself to have fallen irretrievably in love. Mavis says he told his friends and family he would have no-one else or Hector Angus Moles was not his name. What a beautiful story.'

Aunt Hilda mopped her eyes with an embroidered handkerchief. 'I am becoming emotional just repeating it.'

'Weddings can do that,' Alice agreed, thinking this was not the case for her. 'Can I talk to you, Aunt Hilda?'

'Of course you can. What is it, my dear?'

Alice led the way into the parlour where the remains of the afternoon tea was still on the doilied table. The sherry decanter stood there too along with two small stemmed glasses.

'I'll call for Maggie to clear this up,' Hilda said.

'Can't it wait for a moment?' Alice said. 'I need to speak to you.'

'Very well,' Hilda looked surprised at her impatience, 'Let's take a seat and discuss what is on your mind. I can see you are quite agitated.'

Alice launched in straight away. The words tumbled out easily because she had gone over them in her head again and again.

'I can't bear the thought of marrying Charles. I know you dislike him intensely too. In fact, I'm afraid of him and I suspect you are too. But I'm in love with someone else and we want to marry. Oh, Aunt Hilda, please say you'll help us. I know you want the best for me. Will you speak to Father?'

Alice congratulated herself on saying all that had to be said, until she noticed the horrified expression spreading across her aunt's face.

'You foolish girl, what have you done?' Aunt Hilda gasped.

'You must understand — '

'I understand nothing. Who do you think you are in love with? Where did you meet him? I pray you have done nothing inappropriate?' Aunt Hilda wailed. 'Your mother will blame me. Phyllis too. Oh, what have I done to deserve this?' She clutched at her pendant as if it could save her.

'Keep your voice down!' Alice whispered frantically. She couldn't bear it if the servants heard.

'Don't dare to tell me what to do, when you have sullied the family's name,' Aunt Hilda snapped and then burst into tears.

Alice was at a loss to know what to do. She had expected her aunt to support her and be happy for her. She had fondly imagined them sitting with their heads cosily together, working out what to say to Alice's parents so that she and William could marry. She had not imagined this, where Aunt Hilda sobbed her heart out and looked frightened.

She pushed her handkerchief into Hilda's shaking hands. 'Please don't cry. I'll tell you everything but we must be quiet in case someone overhears. Please, Aunt Hilda, you must be quiet.'

Hilda's sobs subsided until she was hiccuping and blowing her nose into Alice's favourite hanky. Alice grimaced. A boil wash would be necessary.

'Tell me, then,' Aunt Hilda said, finally. 'If you have allowed some unknown man to … to dishonour you, then I cannot help.'

'It's not like that. His name is William Morrow.' Alice explained the whole story. When she was finished, she sat back and waited.

Aunt Hilda was pale. She unstoppered the sherry decanter and poured a generous amount into one of the glasses. She lifted it to her lips and drank it in one gulp.

'It's medicinal,' she said, before Alice could comment. 'I feel a little better for it but you've given me a terrible shock. With your mother away in London, I am in charge of you. Your father isn't here on a daily basis. It's up to me to see that you are safe in body and spirit and that you are taught your morals. I've failed.'

'You haven't failed,' Alice exclaimed, 'If anyone's failed, it's Father. After all, I wouldn't have met William if he hadn't taken me with him to the shipyards.'

Aunt Hilda frowned. 'That's a feeble excuse, indeed. The blame must then be entirely on your own shoulders. Your mother brought you up well and I have endeavoured to do the same.' Her cheeks were a rich pink as the sherry took effect and gave her strength.

'Will you help me?' Alice asked. She lowered her gaze and gripped the folds of her long skirt in hope.

'It's impossible. You are promised to Charles and the wedding is only a matter of months away. There is no way of changing that without bringing shame to the family, and I know you do not wish for that. You must put your feelings for this young man, William, aside and forget all about him.'

'I can't,' Alice said.

An unusual determination glinted in Aunt Hilda's eyes as she stared at her niece.

'You must. You will marry Charles and that is that.'

'I thought you'd understand,' Alice said, tears trickling down her cheeks. 'I have no-one else.'

'My dear,' Aunt Hilda said, softly, 'you are not the first nor will you be the last to find yourself in such a predicament. Many a young lady has fancied herself in love but married with the family's approval to another. And most of those young ladies are perfectly contented after a while.'

'How can you know that?' Alice's voice tailed off. 'This happened to you too?'

'I didn't marry your Uncle Tobias, rest his soul, for love. But I came to love him as you will learn to love Charles.'

'I'll never love him,' Alice said. 'I'll be miserable forever.'

'There is nothing we can do except accept the future. Now, I must call for the maid.'

Maggie appeared so quickly that Alice had an awful feeling that she had been listening outside the door. She had a triumphant air to her as she swept away the glasses and crockery. Aunt Hilda said nothing but stared out the window and Alice pretended to look at her embroidery circle which she had left on the couch.

* * *

Lizzie turned on her heel and stared back the way she had come. There was no-one there, or at least, no-one suspicious. The pavement had a reasonable

212

number of people walking along, staring into shop windows or stepping in and out of the carriages and trams that ran along the wide street. She had picked up Alice's gloves at the milliner's shop and was now on her way to the doctor's house to pick up the medicines. She had the sense that someone was following her but couldn't see him or her. She reached the doctor's house in a leafy lane tucked behind the main street.

'Miss Whittaker's medicine, please,' she said to the maid who answered the door.

'Just a moment, miss,' the girl said.

Lizzie's back prickled with a sensation of being watched yet when she glanced around, there was nobody there.

'You're being daft,' she told herself.

'Sorry, miss?' The maid was back with a paper bag of clinking, glass bottles.

'I was — listen, do you see anybody?'

'What do you mean? I see you.'

Lizzie looked at the maid's dull eyes and bucked front teeth and managed not to roll her eyes.

'Of course you see me. But can you see beyond me? Is there someone else?'

The maid peered over Lizzie's shoulders. 'Sorry, miss, it's all a bit blurry. I'm short-sighted, see. My granny was the same at my age. Can't see to lace my boots in the morning.'

'Never mind, then. Thanks for the medicines.' Lizzie counted out the coins and put them in the girl's palm.

She decided to take a different route back to the Whittaker house. One that involved winding back streets. Whoever it was, she could lose him there. She walked quickly, not afraid but wary. There were incidents where young women were attacked in the city and their money and goods taken. Or worse, they were the target for violence. Lizzie had only a few coins left after paying for the medicines and the gloves.

Her boots clattered over the cobblestones, making too much of a racket. Lizzie winced at the sound. She began to walk faster, glancing back every few steps. Then she broke into a run, up a steep path which made her gasp. At the top, she stopped, with a painful stitch in her side. Gasping and rubbing her waist, she glimpsed a figure in dark clothes with a tall hat below. Even as she watched, he vanished into a doorway or lane. She hadn't imagined it all. It was Charles Tunbridge. It had to be. He was very tall and so was the figure she'd seen. It struck her that she was meant to be leaving a note for William in the usual tree. It was impossible now unless she lost the man behind her.

She forged on ahead, trying to lose her shadow by ducking into side streets and curving back onto other roads. Her head was full of thoughts. Alice had been right. Charles had seen her and William that day by the river. It made sense, otherwise why was he following her now? He must be suspicious of Alice. He had Maggie watching her in the house. He must guess that Lizzie knew her mistress's secrets. Had he followed her before? Her mind raced as fast as her legs as she ran towards the Groveries. Convinced, at last, that she had lost him, Lizzie took a deep breath to recover. Her lungs felt raw from the running. She headed to the Canadian Pavilion and slipped the note into the hole in the tree, standing on tiptoe to do so. A little boy, dressed in a navy sailor suit, stared at her. She stuck her tongue out and he giggled and ran away.

She walked away. She was almost at the entrance to the Exhibition when she bumped into someone. Apologising, she looked up straight into Charles Tunbridge's expressionless face. He tipped his hat to her.

'It is I who must apologise, Miss MacDonald. I do hope I haven't hurt you. It is Miss MacDonald isn't it? Your father works at the gondolas' boat house?'

Lizzie's stomach lurched. 'You keep away from my family.'

'Or you'll do what exactly?' His tone was debonair and polite.

'Too many folk around to threaten me properly?' she said. 'In that case, I don't have to hang about to hear what you say.'

'Suit yourself.' He paused as she pushed past him. 'Tell Alice I'll be calling on her soon. Perhaps she'd enjoy a visit to the Canadian Pavilion.'

Lizzie felt cold. She kept going, not wanting to give him the satisfaction of seeing that he'd unnerved her. He knew. He knew about Alice and William. What was going to happen now?

* * *

In the end, Lizzie didn't tell Alice. She was fretting about her conversation with her aunt earlier in the day. It was after supper and Henry Whittaker had gone to his club. The two girls were upstairs in Alice's room.

'Oh, Lizzie, I shouldn't have told her. She has one of her migraines and is lying down in her room. It's my fault. I thought she'd be on my side.'

'She is on your side. But she won't have you ruin yourself.'

'My life will be ruined if I have to marry Charles,' Alice wailed.

217

Lizzie shrugged helplessly. Charles was hateful but he was rich. There were worse lives.

'You must calm down. You'll make yourself ill again,' she said, taking Alice's arm and guiding her to the bed. 'I'll help you undress and give you a sip of the tonic. That'll make you sleep.'

It took an hour of reading before Alice slipped into sleep. With a sigh, Lizzie put the book down. The house felt lonelier than ever. She had a desperate longing to be home with Ma and Dad, Donald and Iona. It might be shabby lodgings in a single makeshift room but it was filled with love and affection. Here the large house was silent. The servants were downstairs, finishing their tasks for the day before they had a few brief hours to themselves.

Lizzie went down to the kitchen, intending to get a drink and have a chat to Emmie. The younger girl had blossomed with Lizzie's friendship. At least she wasn't completely alone. That cheered her. She went in to the kitchen with a smile. She stopped. Emmie wasn't there but Cook was. She was stirring milk in a pan. The sweet, creamy smell was enticing. Cook turned.

'I'm getting a glass of water,' Lizzie said hastily.

Usually, Cook looked at her as if she was a dirty rag blown in. Tonight, however, she smiled. The sight of her peg-like teeth with a gap at the front was unsettling.

'I'm making hot chocolate. You'll take some with the rest of us?'

'Yes, please.' Lizzie hesitated. 'What's changed?' she asked, boldly. 'You never offer me any.'

The older woman flushed and stirred the milk pan vigorously before answering.

'Happen, I've not been fair to you.'

'What's changed your mind?' Lizzie wasn't going to make it easy for her. She'd had months of feeling isolated and disliked. 'Is it Emmie?'

'Emmie?' Cook sounded surprised. 'What's it do with Emmie? My good friend, Fiona, today told me she knows your family.'

Lizzie, in turn, was surprised. Ma must've walked that very afternoon over to the house where Fiona MacDougall worked as a cook. Knowing how slowly Ma walked and how much pain it would have caused her, Lizzie felt a pang of love for her mother. She hadn't wasted a moment to try to help Lizzie.

'That's it then?' Lizzie said. 'Fiona MacDougall says she knows my mother, and all's well.'

Cook sniffed. 'You can take the good fortune or leave it the way it is. What's it to be?' She poured the hot milk into a jug and added the cocoa powder, avoiding Lizzie's eyes.

'What I want to know is what I did wrong when I came here. Why did you all take against me in the first place?'

'It was wrong of us. I admit it. Maggie said you were lazy and dirty in your ways and we believed her. I know better now. Fiona says your ma is a hard worker and looks after her family. Lizzie, lass, can we move on?'

Lizzie waited a moment. She was furious with Maggie but she'd known already that the maid hated her and wanted to make her life unpleasant. No doubt egged on by Charles Tunbridge.

She forced a smile. She'd been offered a welcome and it was better late than never.

'Yes, let's move on. I'd love a cup of hot chocolate with the others.'

'Pick up that jug and tray then. Follow me.'

Later, she lay in her bed in the attic room, listening to Maggie's snores in the bed next to hers. Maggie was as horrible as ever. Lizzie had enjoyed seeing her annoyance as the other servants thawed to her. They had taken their cue from Cook, even Mrs Kearns. Emmie was delighted and kept grinning and winking at Lizzie from her seat opposite at the big wooden dining table. In their shared room, Maggie ignored her as usual. Lizzie didn't care. She had a full stomach of hot chocolate and shortbread fresh from the oven. She replayed the conversations from downstairs. She'd even been asked what she thought about various topics. John, the footman, had flirted a little as they all filed out after. Not that she was interested. Jamie was the only man for her.

The thought of Jamie going across an ocean made her roll on her side and curl up her knees to her chin. She'd miss him something awful. It would be as if her heart was ripped out. There were only two months to go until the International Exhibition closed its gates for the last time. She didn't know how she'd bear it. She fell asleep with his name on her lips.

10

'Another spoonful, please, Lizzie,' Alice demanded sleepily.

Lizzie looked at her. Alice's eyes were heavy-lidded with purple shadows underneath. Her wispy hair was dishevelled from a night's tossing and turning and she smelt of sleep and sweat.

'Are you sure you haven't had enough already?'

Alice nodded. 'I've been feeling much better lately since taking this medicine. I'm calmer and things don't bother me so much. Even Charles seems nicer. Perhaps I imagined him being so horrible.'

Lizzie's eyebrows rose. 'That's powerful stuff if it can make you forget his attack on you.'

Alice swallowed the liquid and licked her lips. 'Is it possible I over-reacted? I feel so ... peaceful towards everyone. Aunt Hilda's right.'

'What did she say?'

223

'I told you a fortnight ago.' Alice sounded impatient. She rubbed her face. 'Didn't I? That I have to marry Charles or bring shame to the family.'

'And you've accepted it now?' Lizzie asked, hoping her friend had.

Life was going to be complicated if she kept seeking William out. Who knew what Charles was capable of?

'I think so. I can still meet William as a friend. In fact, I must arrange another meeting soon so I can tell him as I haven't managed to see him since then. You'll take a note for me today.'

'Of course.'

'And you don't need to hurry back. Go and see Jamie afterwards, if you wish.'

Lizzie hesitated, water jug in hand. She hadn't told Alice yet about Charles accosting her near the Canadian Pavilion. Was it right to worry her? Especially when she seemed to have accepted her forthcoming marriage. Although, Lizzie doubted it would be a happy union.

When Lizzie was present, it irritated her that Alice acquiesced quietly to

Charles's commands and never contradicted him. She saw how it pleased Charles and how his arm on Alice's moved her along like a puppet on a string. Alice's aunt was eager to please him too now that the wedding was not far off. Lizzie noticed she kept her eye on her niece as if afraid Alice would turn tail and run. She thought it was a mistake for Alice to tell Hilda about William. The only good to come out of it was that Alice hadn't sent any notes for ten days or more and so Lizzie hoped Charles had forgotten about his rival or believed it to be over.

Lizzie hurried across to the Groveries with a message from Alice to tuck into the secret hole in the tree. It was a cold October day with a cold breeze and the first leaves of autumn kicking up from the paths. Another month and all these wonderful displays, music recitals, football games and even the buildings themselves must be gone. It was impossible to imagine.

Lizzie had intended to go from the

tree then to the boathouse but there was a note in the tree already. She knew Alice would want to read it immediately. With a sigh, she took it swiftly into her palm where no-one could see it. She'd have to visit Jamie later. The wind whipped through her thin dress as she walked back.

She found Alice in the front drawing room reading a letter. When she saw Lizzie, she put it down on the silver platter beside her and looked expectant.

'You've got a message from William?' she whispered, although they were alone in the room.

'Here it is.' Lizzie passed it to her and waited, in case there was a message to take back.

Alice read it quickly and smiled. 'He's working at the Exhibition this afternoon. How perfect. I can see him and no-one will be suspicious. He writes that he is to be in the Machinery Hall where the ships' engines are displayed and there are design drawings on show. His job is to answer any questions the public may have. I wonder if my father will be there too. I don't need to write an answer. I can simply go there after luncheon. I don't need you now, you can go and help the maids.'

When Lizzie had left, Alice picked up the letter she'd been reading. It was from her mother.

Darling Alice
How are you keeping? I do hope that you are quite well again. I am pleased that you are looking forward to marrying Charles and that you enjoy his company to the various tea shops and for gentle walks. I enjoy your letters with all your news. The Exhibition does sound quite marvellous and I am sorry that I have missed out on all its wonders.

You must not worry about the wedding arrangements. Between Mrs Kearns and your Aunt Hilda, everything is quite in order and nothing has been forgotten. Please remember to have your wedding dress re-fitted in case you have gained weight. For some reason, Hilda does not want to raise this with you as it will make the wedding all too real. I have told her that the wedding is indeed 'real' and that in another two months you will be Mrs Charles Tunbridge with all the wealth and prestige that will bring.

Your aunt wants the wedding to go well and so do I. Sadly, your Aunt Phyllis's leg has not healed as quickly as we had hoped and my services are still required here. By the time you receive this letter, I had hoped to be packed and ready to return home. But we must be patient. I shall certainly have returned in time for the wedding. I look forward to seeing you and your father.

Your loving mother.

Alice grimaced. She had avoided trying on her wedding dress so far. But she couldn't duck out of it forever. Aunt Hilda had mentioned it faintly this very week but Alice had ignored her. It was lovely that Mother was coming home before the wedding but she'd expect the dress to be fitted and ready. Despite what she'd told Lizzie, Alice still had some misgivings about marrying Charles. Yes, she was calmer when she met him but she missed William.

She had discovered that if she didn't argue with Charles, life was much more pleasant. It didn't really matter that much which venue they went to. If she suggested Mrs Morgan's Meeting Room and he decided they should go to the roof top café instead, did it matter? At first, she had tried to get her own way. But the foul atmosphere in which they then sat at whichever coffee rooms she'd chosen, meant it was hardly worth it. Charles was capable of sulking for hours. It was much easier to agree to his choice.

His arm guiding her on their walks had at first annoyed her. Yet, if she tried to wriggle free, he simply clamped her more firmly. Alice knew only too well, that his grip was capable of leaving bruises if she protested too much. Now, when they walked out together, she let him steer her as if she had no will of her own. She remembered Aunt Hilda's shock at her confession of loving William. She had no desire to bring shame to her family. If she had to give William up, then painful though it was, it must be done. Somehow, today she had to tell him it was over.

Alice went in search of Aunt Hilda. The older woman was supervising, along with Mrs Kearns, the cleaning out of the linens store. Two maids had the job of airing all the linens, cloths and blankets then cleaning the store room and returning all to its previous neat state. Aunt Hilda's face was flushed with the exertion of giving orders. She looked relieved to see Alice.

'Ah, there you are. Shall we take tea?'

'Mother wishes me to try on my wedding dress.'

'I shall send for Mrs Fort, the seamstress. Send Lizzie with a message, please Mrs Kearns.'

The dress was made of ivory silk. It slipped like cool hands over Alice's skin as she put it on. Aunt Hilda gave a sigh of delight and dismay all in one. Alice could quite see why. Although it was a divine creation with a neat bodice and tiny blue forget-me-nots trimmed to the collar and cuffs, it hung off her frame.

'You've lost weight,' Aunt Hilda reproached her.

'It's been two years since I last wore it,' Alice said, defensively.

She wasn't going to agree with Hilda but she was shocked at how much weight she'd lost over the two years. It wasn't as if she had been large to begin with. She hadn't much appetite these days. She'd heard Cook grumbling about it when she sent dishes back untouched.

'Please take the dress in, Mrs Fort,' Aunt Hilda said. 'It must be perfect.'

Alice stood still as the seamstress, with a mouthful of pins, began to pin and tuck the material. When she had used up the pins in her mouth, Mrs Fort spoke to Hilda with a stern glance at Alice.

'She cannot lose any more weight. The dress won't take it. As it is, I must trim and tuck and perhaps cut. It's a waste of this beautiful material.'

'I'll see to it myself, Mrs Fort. Please do not distress yourself. Alice, you must eat. I will speak to Cook today and you will have a special diet to fortify you. Charles won't wish to marry you if you are but skin and bone. Never a good look on a young woman.'

Aunt Hilda continued to fuss around both women until Alice felt sorry not only for herself but for the harassed seamstress too. She zoned her aunt's rising tones out and stared into the mirror opposite her. She saw a young woman with a haunted expression staring back with grey eyes that were too large for her face and cheekbones which jutted too sharply under her pale skin. Alice found she had to drop her stare. At least the dress was lovely, she thought. A long row of silk-covered buttons ran the length from the embroidered collar down the bodice and almost to the long hemline. There were folds of silk and even lines of soft white feathers at the back of the wedding dress, and a great looped bow. The forget-menots signified true love while their blue colour meant fidelity. She touched them and gave a faint smile. If it was William she was marrying, the little embroidered flowers would mean everything.

'Come along, Alice dear, do stand up tall for Mrs Fort. That's better.'

* * *

The Machinery Hall was situated on the other side of the main road from the Grand Avenue and was reached by a covered walkway. Alice, accompanied by Lizzie, walked across along with a steady stream of other visitors. There was a light drizzling rain and many held umbrellas which added to the difficulty of not being bumped and pushed in the crowds. Alice wore her favourite blue hat, the peacock feathers drooping in with damp. Beside her, Lizzie looked frozen in her thin coat.

Alice decided she'd buy her a good thick winter jacket. If Lizzie's stubborn pride made her reject it, she'd insist.

'What an amazing place,' Lizzie said as the young women passed into the entrance of the Machinery Hall and realised the enormous size of it. 'I came here one day with Jamie but I didn't really take notice we were so busy talking and eating ice-cream.'

'I've never seen such a huge glass ceiling,' Alice agreed, staring upwards. 'However does it stay up?'

'It's so noisy.' Lizzie clapped her hands to her ears.

'It is but we'll get used to it, no doubt,' Alice said. 'All those engines makes such a racket. Now, where is William?'

They stood on a wide central ground with displays of trains, carriages, parts of ships and working engines on either side. Above them on the left and right were raised walkways so that people could view the great machines from above. There was even a real waterfall, with water pumped back in a continuous loop, displaying an engineering feat and promoting the company which had built it.

'Are those ship engines?' Lizzie pointed ahead. 'Let's go there.'

Alice caught her arm. 'Remember you are my chaperone so don't leave me. I want you out of earshot but close enough for propriety.'

'Yes, don't worry. Are you really going to tell William it's all over between you?'

'We never promised each other anything. We knew it was hopeless. I suppose I'm simply reminding him of that,' Alice said sadly. 'I only hope we can remain friends.'

'Will Charles allow you to have male friends?' Lizzie looked doubtful.

Alice groaned, 'I'm so confused these days. My head is foggy and I'm not sure what is done for the best. I know I have to put my own happiness aside if I am to make my marriage work. What else can I do?'

Lizzie shrugged and Alice knew she had no answers either. She realised suddenly that although she and Lizzie were separated by class and wealth, as women they were equally powerless to decide their futures. It was an uncomfortable thought.

There was a great engine with moving parts and a stink of engine oil and coal. In front of it, at a desk spread with large plans and drawings was William.

He was in earnest conversation with a man dressed in a top hat and with a cane. The man's wife looked bored. Alice waited until the couple had moved on before approaching William. Her heart flipped gladly at the sight of his sandy hair and hazel eyes. He had the gentlest features, she thought. He would never try to dominate me or pinch my skin when angry or demand we go walking if he knew I was fatigued.

'Miss Whittaker, how delightful to see you,' William said formally, while his smile lit up his eyes and sent her a secret message.

'Mr Watson. How wonderful. I had no idea that you worked here,' Alice said, as if she was surprised.

William smiled. 'I think it's safe to speak. The noise of the engines will block out what we say. Lizzie can act as a look out and warn us if anyone comes near.'

Alice nodded to Lizzie, who stepped a little apart from the couple. She knew Lizzie wouldn't let them down.

'Why haven't you been here before?' Alice said. 'It is such an easy place to meet and without suspicion.'

'Usually it's my colleagues who are sent. But one has a cold and the other is needed elsewhere today. I'm enjoying the novelty of being away from the shipyards. I had no idea people found drawings and plans so interesting.'

'Indeed,' Alice said hastily, not at all interested in such things. 'How are you? I've missed you so much.'

'And I you,' he said fervently. 'I haven't had a chance to send many messages and it's so long since we last met. Is Charles … is he treating you well?'

'Charles is … ' Alice faltered. 'He is … difficult to deal with but I must accommodate that and prepare myself to be a good wife.'

William's face dropped but he managed a faint smile. 'Of course. It's not as if we can be together. You're right. And, you're very brave. I'm proud of you.'

Tears prickled her eyelids. She searched for her handkerchief and rubbed her nose with a loud sniff.

'I'm sorry,' she said, 'I mustn't make this hard for both of us. I think that we must stop sending messages to each other.'

'You're giving up?'

'We must. Don't you see? There's no hope for us. We're prolonging the agony of knowing we can't be together.'

'I thought we agreed that despite that we'd keep in touch and write to each other?'

'I know that's what we said, but I can't. It's too painful, knowing it's hopeless.' The tears were running down Alice's cheeks and she didn't try to stop them.

William reached out as if he would touch her and then as quickly dropped his hand to his pocket in quiet despair.

'Then there's no more to be said,' he murmured, his gaze fixed on the fine detailed drawings in front of him.

'You should go, Alice. I wish you well in your marriage and I hope with all my heart that you will be happy.'

'William …' Alice whispered, her heart feeling as if it was being torn in two.

He turned away into a room at the back of the engine display. Drying her tears, Alice turned blindly towards Lizzie, feeling hollow and miserable.

'You've done the right thing,' Lizzie said, gently leading her away from the ships' section.

'I know, so why does it feel so wrong?' Alice asked.

★ ★ ★

It wasn't until her Wednesday half day that Lizzie was able to meet with Jamie. Instead of walking around the Groveries

239

which they usually did, he had asked to meet her on the main road at the tram stop.

'Where are we going?' she asked, as he met up with her.

He kissed her heartily, much to the disgust of a woman walking past who threw them a dirty look.

'Wait and see. Here's the tram now.' He let her climb on first and followed her on. 'Two tickets to Stobcross, please.'

'Stobcross? I don't know it,' Lizzie said, as Jamie paid and the conductor gave him two tickets.

'Aye, well, you've a treat in store.'

His face was ruddy from the wind and his eyes danced merrily. He exuded youth and strength and Lizzie was invigorated too. The day was full of possibilities. A whole half day when she wasn't at the beck and call of someone else. If it wasn't Alice asking her to read or draw or sit with her, then Mrs Kearns was never short of tasks for her to do. When she ran out of ideas, Cook stepped in and Lizzie was often peeling great mounds of vegetables. She blew out a contented sigh.

'Alright?' Jamie grinned.

'More than alright,' she laughed up at him. 'Don't let's waste a moment today. I want to enjoy everything.'

The tram, pulled by two strong, chestnut-coloured horses, moved along the busy street. Between the carriages, carts and pedestrians, Lizzie glimpsed the River Clyde, the sunlight glinting off its sluggish grey surface. Seagulls flew overhead and a variety of boats went past while others bobbed up and down on their moorings.

She was conscious of Jamie's leg next to hers. As the tram swayed round curves in the street, she was flung against his body. Every touch felt sensitive as if their bare skin met instead of through layers of clothing. Although the day was bright, the October air was chilly and Lizzie wished she had a thicker coat wrapped around her. She shivered and felt Jamie squeeze her hand. He took his scarf and laid it round her shoulders. She tucked it against her neck gratefully. It had his body warmth and his scent upon it.

'Thanks,' she smiled.

'Can't have you freezing to death before the day's started,' he grinned. 'There's a fair breeze coming off the river today and we'll feel that where we're going.'

'You're still being mysterious,' Lizzie laughed.

Some while later the horses stopped and Lizzie, Jamie and two others got off the tram. They were at the Queen's Dock on the Clyde, and the smell of brine and oil was overpowering along with the noise of men working and machinery clanking. They walked down to the river's edge. An enormous liner was in at the dock side. Lizzie had to crane her neck to see the ship's top decks and the three proud black-painted funnels. A number of gangways and cranes connected the ship to the dock side, looking like a giant network of spider webs. The name City of Rome was emblazoned on her side. A smaller vessel lay at anchor behind it.

The docks were bustling with sailors and warehouse workers. Men and cranes ferried freight cargoes across to the large ship. Lizzie smelt the clean fishy tang of herring and the peaty whiff of whiskey.

'They're taking the herring, whiskey, woollens and other goods on as cargo,' Jamie pointed as overhead, a large wooden container swung from the dock over to the liner.

'Where's the ship going?' Lizzie asked but had already guessed the answer with a sinking heart.

'To New York,' Jamie said and the excitement in his voice could hardly be contained. 'This is the Anchor Line's largest ocean liner. She'll be leaving tomorrow for the eight day voyage, packed with goods and immigrants.'

'What's the Anchor Line?' Lizzie said, feeling ignorant.

Jamie grinned at her. 'It's one of the great shipping companies of the Clyde. Have you never seen their posters? They make you want to jump on a ship and sail away to an exotic land.'

'Which is exactly what you're going to be doing,' Lizzie said, trying to smile.

'Aye, well, my trip won't be so romantic,' Jamie grimaced. 'My ticket's for steerage and I've heard stories from my pal who works as a steward, that it's not much fun. People are crammed in like sardines down in the lower decks and the food's all porridge and stew with pudding only twice a week. Best block your nostrils, he says, as there's not much in the way of washing facilities.'

'Doesn't that put you off going?'

'Not at all. I'm used to worse. Besides, when I get to America, I'm going to be working harder than I ever have before to set myself up on a wee tract of land.'

'Will you be going on this ship?' Lizzie asked, staring at the magnificent liner with the top decks as high up as the sky. There were a few people staring back down from the upper deck railings. A gentleman with a tall hat and a woman beside him with a flowery bonnet and dainty parasol ambled along the deck.

Jamie shook his head. 'Not this one.

My ticket's for the SS Astoria. She's a smaller liner with two funnels. She takes two hundred saloon passengers on the upper decks and seven hundred steerage passengers below. There's a weekly service to New York on Thursdays and I'm booked for the fourteenth of November.'

'That's only five days after the Exhibition closes,' Lizzie blurted out in dismay.

'There's no point me waiting around as I won't be paid,' Jamie said. 'Look at this smaller boat. Do you know what it's for?'

Lizzie shook her head, feeling increasingly miserable. Why had Jamie brought her here? It was as if he wanted to rub her nose in the fact he was leaving. She would never see him again when he went to America. Was this outing really supposed to be a treat? A flicker of anger rose up in her chest. It was fun for him but he didn't seem to care that he was leaving her behind. Conveniently forgetting that it was she who had suggested that they enjoy the summer and not commit to each other, Lizzie let her anger fizz and grow.

'This is the Anchor Line's tender,' Jamie was explaining, gazing at the ship and oblivious to Lizzie's mood. 'She's used to ferry passengers from Glasgow to the Tail o' the Bank at Greenock and the waiting liners if the weather's too poor or the tide won't let the ships get here to the port.'

Lizzie wasn't listening any more. She'd stoked her anger and now it burst out of her.

'Why did you bring me here?' she cried. 'What kind of day out is this? Do you want to torture me with your plans or are you just the most selfish man on earth?'

Jamie looked as shocked as if she'd reached over and slapped him. Lizzie thought about doing just that.

'What's the matter?' he said, at last, as she stood there, fists clenched, heart pounding and head swirling with emotion.

'What do you think's the matter?' she shouted back at him. 'All you can talk about is leaving. You don't even sound the least bit sad to be leaving me. No, you're excited like you can't wait to go.'

She couldn't see him properly now through a blur of tears which dampened her cheeks.

'Aww, Lizzie, I'm sorry,' he said helplessly, 'I never thought — we agreed we weren't courting. I told you plainly that this is my dream and that I can't give it up for anyone, even you.'

Lizzie nodded miserably. 'That you did. You never promised otherwise. We're not courting, I know we agreed on that. But I'm going to miss you something awful.'

She swiped at her wet face angrily. Jamie took a step towards her but the sympathy on his face was too much. She shook her head and moved back.

'No. Leave me be. I need to be alone.' She turned on her heel and ran from the docks, past the working men and the cranes and cargoes, until she was on the street once more. She didn't wait at the tram stop in case Jamie followed her. Instead, she began to walk quickly back towards the west end of the city.

Her anger was gone, replaced by a feeling of humiliation. How could she face him again? She'd poured out her soul along with her tears. She'd made herself vulnerable, had almost begged him to stay. What must he think of her? The problem was that she was in love with him. Lizzie stopped stock still on the pavement. She was in love with Jamie. What had begun as attraction had gradually strengthened into what she knew in her gut was a forever kind of love. She groaned. She had fallen in love with a man she could never have. A man who didn't love her enough to give up his dream of a new life on a far continent.

'I won't see him again,' she told herself. 'It'll be easy enough if I keep away from the river when I'm at the Groveries with Alice.'

That decision should have made her feel better but she felt hollow inside. She reached the Whittakers' house after a long walk and made her way inside. She wanted nothing more than to hide in her room away from everyone else but was afraid that Maggie might be there. Maggie often stayed at the house on her afternoon off. She didn't appear to have another home to go to. Instead, Lizzie went through to the kitchen. Cook had turned out to be a chatty woman with a fount of interesting tales and local gossip. She was generous with the cakes and pies too now that she had taken Lizzie into her heart.

'You're back early,' Cook said with a smile.

She pushed a plate of shortbread across the table. 'Here, sample these. They're freshly made. I've sent a batch up for the Missus and Miss Alice. Though goodness knows that young lady eats like a proverbial sparrow. Half that plate will be sent back down. Is there something the matter?'

Lizzie rubbed at her face and tried to smile.

'The wind was making my eyes water, that's all.'

'If you say so,' the older woman said wryly. 'I won't pry. Now, I'll have to get along with preparing for dinner. Where's that Emmie got to? Emmie! Emmie! Get in here, useless baggage and peel the tatties.'

'I'll give you a hand,' Lizzie said, as Emmie scurried in looking scared.

Keeping her hands occupied helped keep her mind off Jamie. She helped Cook and Emmie make the dinner for upstairs and for the servants later. A maid arrived to take the dishes to the dining table where Hilda and Alice were eating alone, Mr Whittaker having gone to his club to dine. Cook refused Lizzie's offer to serve, telling her to make the most of her half day off as tomorrow would come only too soon.

Lizzie sat alone in the kitchen at the table after the servants' dinner, her fingertips touching the rough scores in the wood from years of knives slipping and cutting into the grain. Cook had gone to speak to Mrs Kearns about the next day's menus, the maid was upstairs clearing dishes and Emmie had been sent to scrub the pantry. The other servants were on duty upstairs, wishing it was time to finish so they could put their tired feet up and rest.

There was a knock at the back door. Before Lizzie reached it, there were another three knocks getting louder and more frantic. She opened the door and Iona fell inside. Lizzie caught her little sister and steadied her.

'Iona, what are you doing here?' she asked, shocked.

'You have to come,' Iona panted, her chest rising and falling in agitation. 'You have to come with me, Lizzie. It's the boat house. It's on fire!'

11

Lizzie grabbed her winter coat and followed an impatient Iona out the kitchen door. It was dark and cold outside and the two girls shivered as they ran down the street and into the park. Their way was lit by street lights but within Kelvingrove Park, the Groveries were closing for the day and the grand illuminations were being steadily put out.

Luckily there was a full moon which cast enough pale light for Lizzie to see where her feet were going.

'What happened?' she said as they hurried along towards the river.

'It's all gone up in flames,' Iona cried, keeping pace with her. 'Freddy and Jamie are getting buckets of river water to put it out. Hurry, Lizzie!'

She came to a halt at the end of the river path as the jetty came into view. Despite the darkness there was an orange glow and the crackle of wood burning.

Figures were lifting buckets and throwing water at the boat house. Lizzie ran down to the jetty. A man was filling buckets while others formed a chain passing them up the line to douse the flames.

'Let me help,' she called.

'Fill up some buckets and pass them on,' came the terse reply.

She set to work, feeling her muscles ache with the heaviness of the full buckets. Before long her skirts were soaked from the slopping water but she kept filling them, her feet in the river. Her feet didn't feel the cold. She concentrated on her work, wondering where Jamie was and glad not to have to face him. Poor Freddy, she thought. How would he manage if the gondolas were destroyed?

Iona appeared beside her.

'I'll help,' she said.

'These are too heavy for you,' Lizzie panted. 'Stay back.'

'Jamie's up there with Freddy.' Iona pointed back at the burning structure.

'Their faces are all sooty.'

Lizzie looked over at the boat house. It looked as if the flames were going out. A pall of grey smoke streamed upwards and the air smelt of ashes and bonfires. Soon, the chain of men with buckets stopped in their task. The fire was out. Tired faces, streaked with ash and sweat, were rubbed and men patted Freddy on the back as they dispersed back to their own businesses. She heard him call his thanks. Jamie emerged from the shadows and she saw him murmur something to Freddy. Both men turned to look at her.

'Grazie, Lizzie,' Freddy said, reaching her. His face and arms were blackened. 'Thanks for helping.'

'Iona came and got me,' Lizzie explained, only too conscious of Jamie's presence behind Freddy. She couldn't meet his gaze, the events of the afternoon were still too raw. She was angry at him and embarrassed with herself. She was determined to ignore him.

'I've already given Iona my gratitude,'

Freddy said, with a tired smile.

'Gratitude?' Lizzie didn't understand.

'She raised the alarm,' Freddy said. 'If she hadn't been so quick the damage would be much greater.'

'I saw him, Lizzie,' Iona said excitedly, 'I saw the man who set the fire.'

'It wasn't an accident?' Lizzie said, appalled.

'It was set deliberately,' Jamie said. He sounded exhausted and his eyes were sad as they sought hers.

Lizzie kept her gaze on Freddy. If she looked at Jamie, if their gazes locked, she had no idea what her heart would do.

'But who would do such a thing?' Even as she posed the question, Lizzie knew.

'A big, tall man,' Iona piped up.

'Did he see you?' Lizzie said.

Iona shrugged. 'Don't know.'

Lizzie's stomach twisted painfully. If the culprit was Charles Tunbridge and he had seen Iona, would he seek revenge on her for spoiling his plans? She was gripped by fear for her little sister. Freddy touched her arm gently.

'You have an idea who it might be,' he said. 'But it's late and we're all tired. The boat house can be saved, Grazie Dio, so I suggest we meet tomorrow to discuss.'

Lizzie nodded. She needed time to mull it over. She had to protect Iona at all costs. And she needed to tell Alice what her fiancé had done now. She took Iona's hand and they waved goodbye to Freddy and Jamie before setting off for home. The main gates were closed to visitors when they reached the entrance but the guard let them through. There was a stream of workers and entertainers heading through glad the day was over and ready for a late meal and their beds.

'Why are you out so late?' Lizzie turned to Iona. 'Does Ma know where you are?'

Iona blushed. 'I sneaked out after I went to bed. Ma and Dad don't know I'm here. Please don't tell them, I'll get into terrible trouble.'

'Why did you do it?'

'The river children go down there late. There's a broken railing they showed me in the woods so you can slip in and out without being seen. It's fun there when it's dark. The water looks spooky and we tell ghost stories.'

'Only tonight you got more than you bargained for.' Lizzie shook her head. 'Oh, Iona, you mustn't do that. What if something happened to you? Promise me you won't do it again.'

'If I hadn't been there, Freddy's boat house would've burned to the ground,' Iona argued.

'Did you see the man's face? Would you recognise him again?'

'I didn't see him clearly but I know he was tall. He was a gentleman, not a working man like Dad or the Russians.'

'How do you know?' Lizzie gripped Iona's hand tightly, thinking of the danger she had unwittingly been in.

'His coat, silly. He had a coat like the gentlemen that come to the café to take tea with the ladies. Not a working man's jacket.'

'You are clever,' Lizzie grinned.

Iona looked brighter. 'Does that mean

I can keep going to the river?'

Lizzie sighed. 'It means you can see your friends during the day. You can't go after dark.'

Iona scowled. 'You're just being mean.'

'If you think I'm being mean, try and see what Ma does to you when she finds out where you've been.'

'You won't tell her, will you?' Iona pulled her hand out of Lizzie's grip and hugged her.

'I won't tell her as long as you stop doing it.'

They had reached the MacDonalds' home now and Iona didn't answer. Lizzie watched while her little sister slipped inside the unlocked door before she began the long walk back to the Whittakers' home on the hill.

★ ★ ★

Charles Tunbridge had not escaped the fire scot-free. The flames had leapt up quicker than he anticipated after he'd poured oil along the bottom of the back frame of the boat house and flicked the lit match. A breeze had sent the licking yellow tongues shooting towards him and he'd been hard put to suppress a yell.

Now, he applied salve to the side of his left hand and managed to tie the ends of a bandage over it. He felt again the excitement of the moment and savoured the smell of burning wood, the sight of the glowing fire and the sound of crackling, disintegrating boards. His heart rate was still high as he relieved it. He had got away with it. It was a fine diversion from the boredom of everyday life and had the additional bonus of punishing the red-haired maid.

If only the alarm hadn't been raised so soon, he might have razed the wooden building to the ground. As it was, he could only hope enough damage had been inflicted to put the girl's father out of work for good.

She only had herself to blame. He'd warned her to stop interfering between him and Alice. Instead, he had seen her with his own eyes, leading Alice across to the Exhibition's Machinery Hall. He had followed them, careful not to be seen. He needn't have bothered with so much caution as the pair of them had gazed only in front and upwards, seemingly in awe of the place. With mounting rage, he watched from a distance as they walked in a beeline to one of the stalls where a sandy-haired man greeted them.

It had been easy enough to wait and find out who Alice's lover was. He had simply ambled past and glanced in to the stall. There, head bent over a large sheet of engineering drawings, was William Morrow. Charles's fury could hardly be contained and it cost him every bit of self-control to amble on, a polite smile on his lips to passers-by when what he really wanted to do was leap inside the stall and beat the boy to the ground.

He knew William worked at the ship yards. He had a good memory for faces and names, especially those who worked for his father. He'd never had need to speak to their young employee directly. Alice had tainted herself with a mere weed of a man. How dare she defy him. He had thought her cowed. She was acquiescent to his demands when they met. How was it possible that underneath she was rebelling? She was a devious, unfaithful woman and she deserved to know that.

He seethed, letting none of it show until he reached the privacy of his rooms at home. There he had paced, plotting how to punish them. It wasn't enough to sack William from his position. No, he and Alice could wait until he thought of some suitable revenge. He'd start with her interfering, annoying maid. Hit her where it hurt. Her family. He'd seen the fear on her face when he hinted he knew where her father worked. She might be stupidly brave when it came to her own safety but it was a different matter if he was to strike at those she loved.

The pain in his hand was distracting. Charles growled as his burnt flesh throbbed and when he thought of Alice. She was his possession and he wasn't used to his belongings having minds of their own. She must learn.

12

'Did you enjoy that?' Donald grinned at Iona, who was skipping along between him and Anna, holding their hands.

'I loved it,' she laughed, lifting an excited pink face to the sky. 'The dancing bear was my favourite, he growled so much.'

'What about the Cossacks? Weren't they marvellous?' Lizzie said, smiling at her little sister as she walked alongside Donald.

'They looked so fierce,' her brother said, pushing his new spectacles up onto the bridge of his nose.

He let go Iona's hand and Lizzie watched as Anna bent down to speak to the little girl and they both laughed.

'She's mellowed,' Lizzie commented with a glance at Donald, as they dropped back to walk behind the other two.

He grinned back at her. 'She's not so bad once you get past the barriers.'

'Not so bad,' Lizzie mocked him gently, 'I thought you might say more of the woman you're going to marry.'

'Aye, she's bonny and fine and I love her,' Donald said proudly. 'She insisted on taking me to the doctor and paid for it too, out of her earnings. I wasn't too proud to say no, I was that worried about my sight.'

'You should have told me or Ma,' Lizzie said, wishing her brother hadn't kept his fears to himself.

Donald shook his head, 'It wasn't fair to burden you and we didn't have enough to pay for a doctor ourselves, did we. Anyway, it turned out I had an infection which has cleared up and I needed glasses for short sight. Now I can see perfectly.' He shoved the spectacles up onto his nose again. 'As long as I can get them to fit.'

'What will you do when the Exhibition finishes?' Lizzie asked.

'I'll go south to London with Anna and Harry. I'll miss you all but Harry can give me work and we'll have a place to start our married life together. What about you? Will you and Jamie give it a go?'

'I've been a fool over him and I need to tell him sorry,' Lizzie said. 'And I want to see if the boat house has been saved. Dad said he still had a job, so that's hopeful.'

'You haven't been down to look for yourself?'

'It's only been a day, Donald. I'll go over now.'

Lizzie felt guilty for having delayed but she argued to herself that it had been important to finally take Iona to see the Russian show after promising it for so long. The truth was she didn't know how to face Jamie again. Freddy would wonder why she'd stayed away and it was only right that she go and see him, she thought.

She left Donald, Anna and Iona at the dairy farm choosing ice-creams despite the chilly autumn day and found the river path to the boat house. Summer blouses and delicate parasols were replaced with fur-trimmed bonnets and woollen and velvet coats these days she noticed as she passed people strolling along the river banks. Her own coat felt very necessary and she buttoned it up to her neck.

She smelt fresh paint before she got to the boat house. Freddy and Jamie were painting newly fitted wooden boards at the back of the building. They put down their paint brushes as she approached.

'As good as new.' Freddy gestured at their hard work. 'Everyone has pitched in to rebuild and the gondolas are still running. We've been lucky.'

'Thank goodness,' Lizzie said with feeling. 'Jamie, can I see you for a minute please?'

Freddy winked at Jamie and nodded at him to go. Lizzie threw him a grateful smile. Jamie came to join her on the path and Lizzie led them away from Freddy so she could speak to him.

'I wanted to apologise,' she said. 'I was wrong to lash out at you the other day at the docks. It's not your fault you're going to America. It's my fault for caring too much.'

'You've nothing to say sorry for,' Jamie said, smiling now that she'd spoken, 'I should be sorry for opening my big mouth without thinking that day. Friends again?'

Friends. Except she could never just be friends when she was in love with him. It was impossible.

'Friends,' she nodded.

He stared at her. 'You could come with me.'

'What?'

'Come with me to America, Lizzie. There are wide open skies and the freedom to make of yourself what you wish. Men make their fortunes there, from rags to riches.'

The enthusiasm in his voice almost persuaded her. The temptation to say yes overpowered her and her lips parted. But reality hit her with a thump. She couldn't leave her family behind.

'I can't,' she whispered. 'I love you but don't ask me to leave Ma and Dad and

Iona. I'd never see them again.'

'You love me?'

Jamie kissed her and she leaned right in to his embrace, loving the warmth and strength of his body against hers. He was comfort and heightened sensation all in one.

'I love you too, Lizzie MacDonald.'

For the moment it was enough. They embraced and kissed until they both drew shuddered breaths of air, their hearts pounding.

'What will we do?' Lizzie said.

Jamie shook his head. 'I don't know. I could stay but my heart's set on the New World and I don't know what I'd do here except work in dead end jobs. You could come but you'd be miserable without your family and you'd end up blaming me or be so homesick you'd leave me.'

There seemed to be no solution to the problem. In silent agreement, they talked no more about it but walked hand in hand along the path, happy in each other's company and glad that their argument was behind them.

★ ★ ★

Glasgow's International Exhibition of 1901 came to a close on Saturday the ninth of November. It was a rainy day but that didn't prevent almost one hundred and eighty thousand people attending in the hope of a last look at the exhibition's marvels and treasures, and the chance to grab a souvenir as a memento of an extraordinary summer. Later, the Exhibition's organisers would calculate that nearly thirteen million people had been there over the six months, coming from all over the world to the second city of the British Empire.

The Whittakers were invited to the grand closing ceremony which took place at the concert hall on the last day at eight thirty pm, with the gold embossed ticket reminding them to be there when the doors opened an hour earlier. Alice had shown Lizzie the ticket.

'Aunt Hilda will attend with Father,' she said, 'I will have to go with Charles on his ticket.'

Lizzie touched the ticket gingerly, hoping her hands were clean enough not to leave a mark on the quality white paper. The gold writing glinted self-importantly.

'You'll have a lovely time. I wish I could go.'

Alice smiled wistfully. 'I wish you could take my place. Or at least come with me. I'm not looking forward to Charles's company. Sometimes...'

'Sometimes what?'

'It's the way he looks at me sometimes when he thinks I don't know. It's ... I don't know ... calculating somehow as if he's judging me.'

'You must be imagining it,' Lizzie said firmly. 'He has nothing to be suspicious of. You gave William up weeks ago and you have been proper in your manners towards Charles.'

Alice glanced about nervously and pulled Lizzie into a corner of her bedroom behind the large potted fern, although they were alone.

'Maggie stopped searching my belongings too.'

'That's good, isn't it?'

Alice pulled at the nearest frond. 'Or he's found out all he needs to know and doesn't need Maggie snooping any more.'

'Most likely he realises you aren't in touch with William any more and is anticipating your wedding. Isn't that more likely?' Lizzie said soothingly.

Lizzie didn't trust Charles either. After the boat house burned, she realised he was capable of terrible things. She couldn't understand why a rich gentleman would stoop to such acts and felt the only explanation was that he was quite mad. Despite that, there was no way out of Alice marrying him and it was Lizzie's job to make sure Alice didn't get anxious.

As it turned out, Alice enjoyed the closing ceremony. She came back to the house where Lizzie was waiting to hear all about it. Her face was flushed and her eyes shone. Lizzie helped her off with her velvet hat and silk shawl and rubbed her hands, cold from the short journey in the carriage.

'Oh, it was marvellous,' Alice sighed. 'Quite wonderful. Mr Walton gave a perfect performance on the organ and there were speeches by dignitaries and delicious light refreshments. I needn't have taken on so with Charles, he behaved in a most gentlemanly manner and was attentive to my needs. I really am very contented.'

'Did your aunt and Mr Whittaker enjoy it?' Lizzie asked politely.

Alice laughed. 'Aunt Hilda fussed before we went about what to wear and what to say and who she might meet. Father said very little but I noticed he wore his best coat and cravat. They were pleased at seeing Charles and I together in harmony, I think. All will be well, I'm convinced of it, Lizzie.'

Lizzie smiled as she helped Alice get into her night clothes and turned down the bed. She moved the warming pan across the bed so that Alice wouldn't be chilled. Maybe all her fears were for nothing. Alice would get married and she'd promised Lizzie to take her with her to the Tunbridge House on the other side of the river and in pretty countryside with fresh, healthy air.

All was quiet for a few weeks. When Lizzie looked out of the windows, she saw that some of the exhibition's buildings had been dismantled while others grew dilapidated in the rain and wind. Marquees and temporary stalls and cafés had disappeared and in the grey gloomy winter days only a few hardy souls walked in the park. It was a contrast to the long, hot and happy summer of activities.

The MacDonalds were still in Glasgow but had moved out of the workers' accommodation into a rented room in a tenement block. Donald had gone to London with Anna and Harry after tearful farewells from them all. Lizzie had had to peel Iona's arms from Donald's waist before he could go. Ma and Dad were debating whether to follow them south. In the meantime, they lived on what small savings they had from the season's work but a decision needed to be made very soon.

Lizzie was torn. She wanted to be with Jamie while he planned to live on the other side of the world. He hadn't gone on the Astoria after all, saying he needed time to think and had managed to delay his ticket. She wanted to be with her family but hated the idea of going down to London. She sighed as she went about her daily work, unable to decide what to do and knowing that time was ticking away. She had the offer of staying to work for Alice but would she be happy in Tunbridge House with Charles's looming presence?

While she was scrubbing some marks off Alice's fur-lined jacket, Alice came and found her.

'Leave that, I need to talk to you,' Alice said, sinking onto the bed and pushing the jacket to one side.

'What can I do for you?' Lizzie asked, wishing she could finish her task in peace, and hoping Alice didn't want read to. Lizzie's reading had greatly improved over the months but she still found it tiring to read out loud.

'I want you to take a message to William.'

'What are you talking about?' Lizzie said, aghast. 'You said it was all over.'

'And it is,' Alice said, waving her hands at her. 'But I must see him just once more before my wedding. Please, do this for me. Take this letter to him. I'll meet him inside the park tomorrow evening when it's dark, for five minutes or so. That's all.'

Lizzie had to do as she was bid but she didn't pretend to Alice that she liked it, or thought it clever. She took a tram over the bridge and walked a little to the shipyard where she waited until the clerks and engineers left for the day. When she saw William, she intercepted him as he walked home.

'I don't think this is wise,' she couldn't help saying, as he read the note eagerly.

'You're right,' William said. 'But Alice has requested I come and I can't refuse her. There can be no harm in a final farewell. Please tell her I'll be there. Thank you, Lizzie.'

The next evening was wet and the

wind came in howling gusts which swept up the dead leaves and small twigs and blew them about viciously. Lizzie peered out of the parlour window and shivered. The raindrops were visible against the street lamps, slanting down and bouncing off the pavements.

'Are you sure you want to do this?' she said, turning to Alice who was busy putting on her blue hat and tying its ribbons under her chin. She had a long, matching blue wool coat which covered her skirts and she was wearing stout leather boots.

'Of course,' Alice said, buttoning the coat up to her neck. 'Aunt Hilda and Father are out at a musical soiree with Miss Christopher and Reverend Moles. Mrs Kearns is absorbed in next week's menus with Cook and the maids will mind their own business. Maggie is sick and gone to her family yesterday. There can be no threat. Now, put your coat on and let us go. William will be waiting.'

'Are you not afraid that seeing William will … undo you?' Lizzie asked, as she put on her own coat and buttoned it up.

Alice had given it to her and it was much warmer and softer than her old winter coat. It was a pretty shade of green and made her red hair flame against it.

Alice looked momentarily tired. 'I love William and I know he loves me. But for better or worse I am affianced to Charles and I know my duty now. I cannot shame my parents otherwise. It's alright, Lizzie. Nothing untoward will happen.'

Lizzie shivered again. 'It's a wicked night. We must take umbrellas.'

The two young women hurried out into the wild evening, stepping away from the solid stone steps of the Whittakers' house across the street and through the railing gate of the top end of the park. Apart from the shriek of the wind, it was quiet. There was a partial moon casting occasional weak shadows between the cloud cover. The rest of the park sloped down and in daylight allowed lovely views over the park land and what had been the exhibition. Now they could vaguely make out the shapes of structures such as the Irish village and the iron fountain with the derelict and half dismantled Palace of Industry a large outline in the background.

★ ★ ★

From a grove of trees, William stepped out. Alice ran to him. Lizzie kept slightly back to allow them some privacy. She felt suddenly uneasy. A prickle of fear tickled at the back of her neck and she looked around. It was difficult to see much in the dark. The street lamps cast a weak yellow glow on the slick wet foliage against the park railings. The nearby shrubs and trees were bending in the wind, slapping wetly onto other trees and shedding twigs and yet more leaves with every movement.

A darker shape moved within a group of trees nearby. Lizzie's chest tightened painfully. She leaned forward, eyes screwed up in an attempt to see clearly.

'Who's there?' she called out.

She glanced back at Alice. She and William were standing with heads close together. She was too far away to hear what they were saying. It only took a brief second to look across at them and then back to the trees but in that instant what she saw took her breath away. Charles Tunbridge stood there and she saw a pistol in his upraised hand.

Then Lizzie was running, almost tumbling as her thick cotton skirts twisted between her legs, feeling as though she was in slow motion, arms out towards Alice and William.

'Run!' she yelled.

Two pale discs of faces turned to her and then all three were running down the hill and into the maze of buildings and detritus of the International Exhibition.

'He's got a pistol,' Lizzie cried as her breath caught in her chest and she panted with exertion.

'We must hide,' William shouted, grabbing Alice's arm and pulling her with him. 'Come on, Alice darling, we must get you to safety.'

Lizzie heard the pounding of their

feet, she smelt the sour damp grass and heard the soughing wind. She strained to hear their pursuer. She felt she couldn't run much further. In the black night amongst the confusion she lost them. She dashed into the mouth of a building and stood for a moment, disorientated. There was a stone pedestal in front of her without a statue and around it, in a circular formation, other shapes. There was a strong stink of rotting plaster. She realised it was the entrance to the Palace of Industry. Beyond her a door sagged off its hinges. The stairway leading up to the cupolas was intact. She remembered it led to salons and cafés.

She ran up it, hoping to hide there and came to an abrupt halt. There was an empty room to her left but straight ahead, briefly illuminated by the moon through the missing roof, she saw that the corridor only went so far before it was torn away and only the wooden beams remained. The workmen were in the middle of bringing the building down bit by bit.

The sound of running feet made her duck into the room on the left until she smelt Alice's perfume and saw the two of them arrive at the top of the staircase.

'Alice,' she said, moving out so they could see her.

'Thank goodness, we lost you,' Alice said, hugging her.

William hovered protectively behind her. What could he do against a man with a gun, Lizzie thought. Even as she thought it, they heard noises below.

'He's here,' Alice whispered.

She gripped Lizzie's arm so tightly it hurt.

'He's unhinged,' William said in a low voice. 'Utterly mad. He was shouting at us as we fled. He intends to shoot all of us.'

'We can't stay here,' Lizzie said. 'It'll be like shooting fish in a barrel.'

'There's nowhere else to go,' Alice said.

'Yes, there is,' Lizzie replied. 'But we'll have to take care. The floor's given way on the corridor but we might pass by walking across the beams.'

Alice gave a low moan of terror. William steadied her.

'We can do this, my darling. We have to. There's no alternative. You're stronger than you think. Isn't she, Lizzie?'

'Yes. You survived pneumonia and you got your health back by being strong. You were strong enough to give William up when it was the right thing to do. Now you can do this. Follow me…and be careful.'

Lizzie led the way as quietly as possible. She was acutely aware of the sounds downstairs of the madman searching for them. She heard him muttering to himself and thought that William was right, Charles had gone completely mad. They had to be fast but make no mistake in their flight to safety. One slip off the beam and they'd fall to the ground floor and death or terrible injury.

Lizzie crept out of the room and turned onto the length of corridor. It was hard to see anything ahead of her as the clouds covered the faint moonlight.

More by sensing than seeing she began to walk along it. Where did the floor end and the gaping beams begin? There! Her foot felt thin air and she pulled back hastily. She felt Alice's breath on her neck before she stepped back to give Lizzie room. They heard a creak of the first step on the stairway below.

'Now!' Lizzie whispered fiercely.

She put her right foot onto the exposed wooden beam. Her leg shook and she willed herself to stay strong. Then her left foot. Now she was balancing. Luckily, although the Palace of Industry was made of wood and plaster, the wood was solid, excellent quality and the beam was reasonably broad. She found her rhythm and balanced on it, like the Indian performers had done that summer high up in the marquee on trapezes and ropes to the gasps of amazement from the audience below.

Now there were no gasps of amazement, no appreciative audience, only the tense rasp of breath behind as Alice and William followed her and the noises of a madman intent on finding them and killing them.

Lizzie made it to the other side and saw thankfully that the corridor continued intact until another flight of stairs down. From memory, that set of stairs would take them down to the courtyard and exits out into the park. If they could make the courtyard they could flee from Charles and get help.

Alice joined her and they watched as William teetered, arms out wide for balance. Beyond him, a dark figure appeared.

'Hurry, William!' Alice screamed.

William made solid ground at same time as there was a loud bellow and Charles Tunbridge launched himself along the corridor in pursuit. In horror they watched as he failed to notice the missing floor and disappeared. The pistol cracked as it went off and there was the sickening thump of a body hitting the ground far below them.

Alice was sobbing hysterically and William tried to soothe her. Lizzie ran to the far stairs and down them to the courtyard. She dashed through one of the doors and came to a stop. It was too late to help Charles. It was obvious from the way he lay that he was dead. She squeezed her eyes shut. It was a pitiful sight and even though he was crazed and dangerous she hadn't wished it to end this way.

Slowly, Alice and William came down to join her.

'What will happen now?' Alice asked.

Lizzie and William exchanged glances.

'Let's get you home,' he said gently.

13

Spring 1902

'I'll miss you so much,' Alice said, tearfully.

'I'll miss you too,' Lizzie said. 'Thank you for the lovely travelling bag and the hat.' She touched the blue hat with its fine peacock feathers where it perched prettily on her head. 'It's your favourite hat, are you sure you want to give it to me?'

'When you wear it, you think of me,' Alice said.

'I will. I'm sorry we'll miss your summer wedding but Jamie's impatient to be on the boat. You will give William our love, won't you.'

'At least I got to see you married.' Alice smiled. 'Are you happy?'

Lizzie laughed. Happy didn't begin to describe her joy in marrying Jamie. The terrible events of that winter night had put everything into perspective. They could so easily have died, either shot by Charles or by falling from the wooden beams of the palace. The following day had been spent talking to the police and to Mr Whittaker who had found it difficult to believe all that had happened.

Finally Lizzie had slipped away to see her family and then to Jamie's lodging house. He had found work at the docks, hauling cargo. It was heavy work and he was exhausted when he got home.

'I'll put the kettle on,' Lizzie said, when he let her in.

His face was streaked with dirt from his day's labouring and he was tired but smiled to see her. 'A cup of tea then.'

'I need to tell you something,' Lizzie said when she passed him a steaming cup of tea. She sat opposite him in the tiny living room and described what had happened the previous night.

'And it made me realise what's important,' she finished. 'If you still want it, I'll come to America with you. Life's too short to wait around.'

'I delayed my ticket to make some decisions,' Jamie said slowly. 'I came to the conclusion this morning that wherever you are is where I want to be. I don't care if we go to America or we make a life here near your family. I just want to be with you.'

Lizzie leaned across to him and he kissed her gently on the lips.

'Oh, Jamie,' she murmured. 'I love you so much. I don't care either. But I'd be pleased to go to America with you. There is a slight condition though … I hope you won't be angry?'

'I can't be angry with the woman I'm going to marry.' He kissed her thoroughly. 'What's the condition? You're making me nervous.'

'I hope you're joking.'

'I'm half joking. Tell me now.'

'How would you feel if my family came too? Dad and Ma are struggling to find decent work and the cold and damp aren't good for her aching joints.'

'I've only had myself most of my life so a ready-made family suits me just fine,' Jamie grinned. 'I've been missing Freddy and his cheerful company since he went back to Italy.'

Lizzie sat back. What Jamie had said had only sunk in. 'Did you propose to me?'

He got off the chair and down on one knee. 'Not properly. Will you do me the honour of marrying me, Lizzie Mac-Donald?'

'Yes, yes, yes,' she laughed. 'Wherever we end up, we'll be happy together.'

'I'm not in favour of a long engagement,' Jamie warned her, 'I want you as my wife as soon as possible.'

★ ★ ★

The details of Charles Tunbridge's death had been hushed up by the families and the authorities. It was reported in the newspapers as a tragic accident with no mention of the chase and the pistol. Alice wore half mourning of lilac over the winter but after firm discussions with her parents and aunt, she was then

289

swiftly engaged to William.

As she told Lizzie afterwards, 'I wasn't prepared to accept other suitors ever. Father clearly felt guilty that Charles turned out so badly and Mama simply wishes me to be happy. As for Aunt Hilda, she cried until Mama told her to stop. Tears of happiness she said, that I should marry for love after all. I suppose she never got to marry the man she loved so she feels for me. Dear Aunt Hilda, her heart's in the right place even if she is rather a fusspot.'

★ ★ ★

A summer wedding was planned and William had already been promoted at the shipyards as befitted Henry Whittaker's future son-in-law. Henry planned to buy the couple a town house in the same street as theirs, overlooking the park.

'Luckily my happy memories of the park and the grand Exhibition far outweigh my bad memories,' Alice said to Lizzie. 'After all, that's where I met you. So I shall be quite pleased to look out the windows of my own home and remember the wonderful months of last year.'

Lizzie took her leave of Alice, looking smart in her new clothes and Alice's beautiful blue hat. She gripped her luggage. Ma and Dad and Iona were already at the dock side, escorted there by Jamie. It was Thursday and the SS Astoria was due to leave that afternoon for New York. Lizzie had detoured to see Alice for the last time. She would always be grateful to her for her friendship and for giving her a place as her maid. She had learnt a lot over the season of the Exhibition and found the love of her life.

Now, she stepped confidently out onto the pavement. She walked down to the main street, through the park with its traces of glory and the fountains playing, the new art gallery proudly in place with its entrance facing where the Exhibition had been.

She'd take a tram along to the Queen's Dock and there, waiting, would be her husband and her dear family. Then they'd walk up the gangway onto the liner and the promise of a new life on the other side of the world.

We do hope that you have enjoyed reading this large print book.

Did you know that all of our titles are available for purchase?

We publish a wide range of high quality large print books including:
Romances, Mysteries, Classics
General Fiction
Non Fiction and Westerns

Special interest titles available in large print are:
The Little Oxford Dictionary
Music Book, Song Book
Hymn Book, Service Book

Also available from us courtesy of Oxford University Press:
Young Readers' Dictionary
(large print edition)
Young Readers' Thesaurus
(large print edition)

For further information or a free brochure, please contact us at:
Ulverscroft Large Print Books Ltd.,
The Green, Bradgate Road, Anstey,
Leicester, LE7 7FU, England.
Tel: (00 44) **0116 236 4325**
Fax: (00 44) **0116 234 0205**

PROMISE OF SPRING

Beth Francis

After the breakdown of her relationship with Justin, Amy moves out of town to a small village. In her cosy cottage, with her kind next-door neighbour Meg, she's determined to make a fresh start. But there are complications in store. Though Amy has sworn never to risk her heart again, she finds her friendship with Meg's great-nephew Mike deepening into something more. Until Mike's ex-girlfriend Emma reappears on the scene — and so does Justin ...

DATE WITH DANGER

Jill Barry

Bonnie spends carefree summers in the Welsh seaside resort where her mother runs a guesthouse. But things will change after she meets Patrik, a young Hungarian funfair worker. Both she and her friend Kay find love in the heady whirl of the fair – and are also are fast learning how people they thought they knew can sometimes conceal secrets. As Patrik moonlights for one of her mother's friends, Bonnie fears that he may be heading into danger ...

ROSE'S ALPINE ADVENTURE

Christina Garbutt

Rose is in need of excitement. Taking a leap of faith, she flies to the Alps to take up the position of personal assistant to Olympic ski champion Liam Woods. Though she's never skied before — or even spent much time around snow — that's not going to stop her! But she hadn't bargained on someone trying to sabotage Liam's new venture ... or on her attraction to him. Can she and Liam save his business — and will he fall for her too?

A BODY IN THE CHAPEL

Philippa Carey

Ipswich, 1919: On her way to teach Sunday School, Margaret Preston finds a badly injured man unconscious at the chapel gate. She and her widowed father, Reverend Preston, take him in and call the doctor. When the stranger regains consciousness, he tells them he has lost his memory, not knowing who he is or how he came to be there. As he and Margaret grow closer, their fondness for one another increases. But she is already being courted by another man …

BLETCHLEY SECRETS

Dawn Knox

1940: A cold upbringing with parents who unfairly blame her for a family tragedy has robbed Jess of all self-worth and confidence. Escaping to join the WAAF, she's stationed at RAF Holsmere, until a seemingly unimportant competition leads to her recruitment into the secret world of code-breaking at Bletchley Park. Love, however, eludes her: the men she chooses are totally unsuitable — until she meets Daniel. But there is so much which separates them. Can they ever find happiness together?